Triple Threat – A Norwegian Forest Cat Café Cozy Mystery – Book 17

by

Jinty James

Triple Threat – A Norwegian Forest
Cat Café Cozy Mystery – Book 17

by

Jinty James

DEDICATION

To my wonderful Mother, Annie,
and AJ

CHAPTER 1

Lauren Denman and her cousin Zoe peered at the pages of the *Gold Leaf Valley Gazette*. Lauren's cat, Annie, a big, silver-gray Norwegian Forest Cat with long fur and a plumy tail, hopped up on the café chair next to them.

"Brrt?"

"Listen to this, Annie," Zoe enthused. *"I hear wedding bells are ringing, and Father Mike is officiating. Who is the lucky lady?"*

"We're reading the new gossip column," Lauren told her fur baby. "Although, I guess it's not that new. It appeared in the newspaper about six weeks ago."

"That's right." Zoe's brunette pixie bangs flopped against her temple in agreement. "Ooh – I bet I know who this is! Ava."

Ava was a local girl who'd been dating the same guy for a few years.

Everyone was happy they were finally tying the knot.

"Didn't someone tell us she was getting married soon?"

"I think it was Brooke." Zoe screwed up her face. "Yeah, I'm pretty sure it was her."

Lauren touched her light brown locks. "I think I should get my hair trimmed soon. It's getting a little long."

"Want me to do it?" After a beat, Zoe giggled.

Lauren met her gaze and realized they were both thinking of the same thing – the time Zoe had cut a little too much off and they'd made an emergency dash to the hair salon, and met Brooke for the first time.

"I'll make an appointment with Brooke later," Lauren replied good naturedly. She checked her white practical wrist watch, her eyes widening. "Is that the time? We'd better open up."

Zoe jumped up and unbolted the oak and glass entrance door.

Lauren glanced around the coffee shop with a sense of pride. Her Gramms had left her this café, as well as the adjoining cottage. Not long after she and Annie moved here from Sacramento and turned it into a cat café – Annie the only feline – Zoe had visited for the weekend, and decided to stay.

The walls were pale yellow, and the furniture consisted of pine tables and chairs. A string-art picture of a cupcake with lots of pink frosting decorated one of the walls – evidence of one of Zoe's hobbies.

Lauren prepared the cupcakes and paninis, and they both made the cappuccino, lattes, mochas, and hot chocolates.

The faint rattle of pastry trays in the commercial kitchen signaled Ed, her burly pastry chef, hard at work. Although Lauren prided herself on her cupcakes and coffee, she knew some of their customers came for his Danish pastries, which were light, flaky, and tender.

A few minutes later, a woman in her late forties entered the café. Dressed in light-weight beige slacks and a rose blouse, she looked cool and comfortable for the spring weather.

"Hi, Cee Cee," Lauren greeted her.

"Brrt?" Annie trotted up to her as she stood by the *Please Wait to be Seated* sign.

"I only have time for a quick to go order today, Annie." Cee Cee Convale smiled down at the feline, her short blonde locks falling forward.

"Brrp." Annie looked disappointed.

"We've just read your latest column." Zoe zipped over to her.

"Did you guess who's getting married?"

"Ava," Lauren replied.

"It was pretty easy," Zoe added.

"You're right." Cee Cee nodded.

"What can I get you?" Lauren asked.

"A large latte and one of your delicious cupcakes, please," Cee Cee replied. "Hmm, I can't decide between your lemon poppyseed or red velvet."

She eyed the glass case where a tempting array of cupcakes awaited.

"Red velvet," Zoe prompted. "The cake crumb is flavored with cocoa and vanilla and just melts in your mouth, and the cream cheese frosting is awesome!"

"How can I resist?" Cee Cee smiled.

"Coming right up," Lauren promised.

"How do you get all the gossip?" Zoe's brown eyes sparkled in curiosity.

"I have my sources." She tapped her nose and laughed. "Gold Leaf Valley might be a small town, but it's amazing how much people talk."

"But you've only been here a short time, haven't you?" Lauren steamed the milk.

"True, but my boss has been here a while, and his wife – that's how I got the job. We used to be in college together, and reconnected after my divorce." She looked pensive for a moment. "Katherine knew I was looking for a job and when the position opened up here for a gossip columnist, she recommended me to her husband." She laughed. "We used to love poring over celebrity news in college."

"I don't think there are any celebrities living around here." Zoe sounded disappointed.

"I like to think that in my column, the local residents are the celebrities." Cee Cee smiled.

"That's a nice way of looking at things." Lauren placed a lid on the cardboard cup and put the red velvet into a paper bag.

"Yeah, ever since you've mentioned Lauren's cupcakes and Ed's Danishes in your column, business has increased," Zoe told her.

"I'm glad. Lauren, do you have a new creation I can mention?"

"Not yet." She felt guilty that she hadn't come up with anything lately. She'd married Mitch, who was a police detective, less than a year ago, and they were enjoying being newlyweds. So was Zoe, with her husband Chris.

"We'll have to think up something so you can put it in your next column." Zoe glanced down at Annie, who'd been listening to the conversation. "Can you think of something?"

"Brrp." *Not yet.*

"How about placing an ad in the paper?" Cee Cee suggested. "Brooke from the hair salon has just put one in, and Gus, the local mechanic, says he's gotten new customers since his first ad with us, and now has a weekly one."

"Really?" Zoe grabbed the newspaper she'd left on the table. Flicking through the pages, she stopped near the back page. "I see it. Ooh, Lauren, he has a used car for sale." Her eyes lit up. "Maybe I've saved enough to buy my own wheels – if it's very cheap."

Cee Cee laughed. "You never know. I'm sure he'll give you a good deal."

"Mitch has taken his car to him for service and was pleased," Lauren remembered.

"A lot of people are recommending him," Cee Cee agreed.

"And the handmade shop has new yarn!" Zoe tapped the same page. "We have to check it out."

"That sounds like fun." Her last knitting project was a red and purple scarf she'd presented to Zoe at Christmas. Perhaps it was time to start something new.

"I'm afraid I have to dash." Cee Cee picked up her treats. "It was nice talking to you. Remember, if you have any gossip to share, let me know."

"We will," Zoe promised.

"I think we should only share nice gossip," Lauren said after Cee Cee had left. "Like Ava getting married, and Father Mike officiating."

"Agreed," Zoe replied.

"Brrt!"

***

The rest of the morning whizzed by in a flurry of customers and the hum of background conversation.

When Mrs. Finch tapped her way into the café, Annie trotted to greet her.

"Brrt!"

"Hello, Annie, dear." Their elderly friend smiled down at the cat, the orange rouge on her cheeks looking like the California poppies she grew in her garden. She wore a fawn skirt and a short-sleeved blue blouse. Her gray hair was caught up in a bun, and wire-rimmed spectacles perched on her nose.

"Hi, Mrs. Finch," Zoe called out. "What can we get you?'

"A nice pot of tea, I think, this morning." She slowly followed Annie to a four-seater near the counter. "And one of your delicious cupcakes, please, Lauren."

"Red velvet, lemon poppyseed, or Norwegian Apple?" She ran through the day's offerings.

"Norwegian apple, dear." Mrs. Finch's eyes twinkled at Annie.

"Brrt," Annie said in approval.

They chatted with Mrs. Finch for a few minutes, as the rest of the customers were enjoying their lattes, cappuccinos, and treats.

Showing her the gossip column, Zoe said, "We guessed who the bride was right away."

Mrs. Finch smiled as she read the small item. "It's Ava."

"You probably know all the gossip around here," Lauren observed, sitting down at the table for a moment.

"You girls might know more than I do, these days." Their friend looked wistful for a moment. "I don't get out that much now."

"But you have phone chats with your pals, don't you?" Zoe asked.

"Yes." Mrs. Finch nodded. "You're right." She smiled. "And I do love coming here."

"And we love visiting you," Lauren replied.

"Especially on craft club night," Zoe added. "We'll be at your house on Friday as usual."

"I'll look forward to it." Mrs. Finch's smile grew. "You must update me on your projects."

"We will," Lauren promised. Now she really *should* check out the new yarn at the handmade shop before Friday.

They stayed at Mrs. Finch's table for a few extra minutes, before more customers entered the café.

Annie seated the newcomers, then returned to Mrs. Finch's table until she was ready to leave. They waved goodbye to their friend, Annie escorting her to the door, and promised to see her on craft club night, if not before.

"I think we should definitely visit the handmade shop after work," Zoe proposed.

"Will they be open after five?" Lauren asked.

"I'll check." Zoe pulled out her phone, her thumbs busy. After a few seconds, she said, "Yes, it's open 'til five-thirty today."

"Okay." Lauren nodded. "Mitch said he has to work late tonight, so he won't be home until seven."

"Chris has a shift this evening." Zoe made a face. "I miss him when he's in paramedic mode."

"Would you like to have dinner with us?" Lauren asked.

Zoe looked tempted, then shook her head. "Thanks, but I should do some more work on my screenplay."

"How's it going?"

"Good." Zoe nodded, as if convincing herself. "It's definitely coming along – I'm just a little stuck at the moment." Her expression brightened. "I know! I think I should organize a script meeting with Annie, Mrs. Snuggle, and AJ. There's a plot idea I came up with after talking to Annie and Mrs. Snuggle a while ago, but I think I really need to see it acted out."

Lauren tried to stifle a smile. "You want the cats to act out your script?"

"Yes." Zoe's brown eyes sparkled. "Why not? I think it will really help me picture it."

"Are there cats in your screenplay?"

"Brrt?" Annie joined them.

"Not yet." Zoe drew in a big breath, excitement flickering across her face. "That's a great idea, Lauren! The princess can have a cat – or maybe she meets a cat – yes! And brings it home and the cat can help her prove her real identity – or something!"

"Brrp?" *Will she look like me?*

"She will now, Annie," Zoe promised.

A while ago, they'd become addicted to watching a movie featuring a princess – all three of them, including Annie. They'd been delighted to discover there was a sequel, and had found out that Father Mike's cat, Mrs. Snuggle, loved watching the films as well. Zoe had come up with the idea of attempting to write her first screenplay – a third princess movie.

Since she'd already explored knitting, crochet, bead jewelry, string-art, and pottery, with her mugs selling well at the café featuring poses of

Annie, she'd decided to try something else. Lauren had to admit that her cousin certainly had a vivid imagination.

Lauren had stuck with knitting, the first craft they'd tried together, and had flirted with sewing, something that made Zoe shudder.

"So I'll call Father Mike and ask him if I can have a playdate with Mrs. Snuggle, and I'll ask Ed the same thing about AJ, *and* we're going to the handmade shop after closing today to check out the new yarn."

"It sounds like you're going to be very busy."

"You mean *we* are going to be very busy." Zoe grinned.

"Brrt!"

CHAPTER 2

"This blue – no, this red – no, this purple." Zoe ran her hands through the skeins of yarn in the handmade shop. They'd hurried there after closing the café at five, and had just made it with ten minutes to spare.

"What about you, Lauren?" the clerk inquired. She'd run the handmade shop for a few years now and took an interest in her customers' projects.

"I love this pale blue." Lauren held up a ball of yarn.

"Good choice." The clerk nodded. "And it's chunkier, so it will be quicker to work up."

"Really?" Lauren looked hopefully at the skein. She was a slow knitter, and didn't always have a lot of time to make something.

"What about that ball of cream next to it?" the clerk suggested. "You could make a two-toned blanket or scarf."

"A blanket," she suddenly decided. The living room had two pink sofas and a pink velvet cushion that Mitch had given Annie a while ago. Although he'd never said anything, she did wonder at times if he thought the room was a little too pink.

"Good idea." Zoe fingered the cream yarn. "Blue and white – I bet Mitch will love it!" She sucked in a breath. "It would also make the perfect baby blanket." Eyeing Lauren's curvy figure, she said, "You're not, are you?"

"Not what?" Lauren furrowed her brow.

"You know." Zoe mimed a big baby bump a couple of times.

Lauren's mouth parted. "No!" She paused. "I don't think so. No. Besides," she lowered her voice, "Mitch and I haven't discussed a timeline yet. What about you and Chris?"

Now it was Zoe's turn to look shocked.

"We haven't really talked about it," she admitted.

"Really?" Lauren looked surprised.

"I think we've mentioned it once, and we both want kids, but I'm not even thirty – yet. There's plenty of time."

Lauren nodded. She was a year older, and she wanted to enjoy time alone with Mitch first. But … maybe she should have a discussion with him about their future family, and how many children they should have, all things going well.

"I don't want to rush you two, but I'm going to close in a few minutes," the clerk warned.

"Sorry." Lauren grabbed two skeins of blue, and two of cream, the yarn soft under her fingertips. She hoped that would be enough.

"We found out about your new stock from your ad in the *Gold Leaf Valley Gazette*," Zoe told her as they approached the counter.

"I'm pleased I took the plunge and did it," the clerk admitted. "Business has picked up already."

"We wouldn't be here right now if we hadn't read about your new yarn coming in," Zoe agreed.

"Will this be enough for a small blanket?" Lauren asked, placing the four skeins on the counter.

"How big do you want to make it?" The clerk scanned each ball, a small beep emitting each time.

"Not too big or I'll never finish it," Lauren admitted.

"Then you might want to make a lap blanket." The clerk eyed the four skeins. "You may need a couple more, but you could see how you go."

"I'll buy them now." She ran back to the small aisle and grabbed two more balls.

"I love all the different colors." Zoe glanced at the baskets of yarn wistfully. "But I'm not crocheting or knitting right now."

"You're writing a screenplay." The clerk smiled.

"How did you know?" Zoe's mouth dropped open.

"I think the whole town is aware by now," Lauren remarked good naturedly.

"I guess ever since the gossip started at Brooke's hair salon a while ago." Zoe giggled.

"Maybe Cee Cee could put it in her column," the clerk suggested.

"Even if most of the town already knows about Zoe's script?" Lauren creased her brow.

"Everyone is aware Ava's getting married, and that was included in the column," the clerk pointed out.

"True." Lauren nodded.

She paid for her yarn, and they said goodbye to the clerk.

Walking back to Lauren's cottage, Zoe said, "We should think about getting our own ad in the newspaper, promoting the café. All the other businesses around here seem to be successful doing it!"

***

The next day, Zoe told Lauren and Annie about her plan while they readied the café for their first customer.

"So, if it's not too busy today, I thought we could close for a few minutes, and run down to the newspaper office, and put an ad in for next week's edition."

"Brrt," Annie said in approval.

"I guess," Lauren replied, thinking of her bank balance – and the café's. Business was okay at the moment but she tried to be careful with expenses. But if the ad brought in more business than it cost, she could make a profit, even if it was a small one.

"I'm sure these ads don't cost much." Zoe waved her fingers in the air, as if reading her mind. "I should have asked the handmade lady yesterday how much it was."

"We can close for a few minutes if it's very quiet today," she warned, not liking to abandon the café even if her reason was business related.

"Awesome!" Zoe smiled.

They finished getting the café ready. Annie strolled around the space, checking that nothing was hiding under the pine tables and chairs, and paying particular attention to each corner of the room.

When Lauren unbolted the oak and glass door on the dot of nine-thirty, she was slightly disappointed at the lack of customers.

"Oops, I forgot to call Father Mike last night." Zoe made a moue. "And Ed." Before Lauren could say anything, she zipped into the commercial kitchen.

She heard her cousin's voice, and Ed's low rumble in response.

"All set." Zoe zoomed through the swinging doors and back to the counter. "Ed says next week would be good for him and AJ as he's only on duty at the animal shelter twice then."

Ed volunteered at the local animal shelter, and his Maine Coon cat AJ accompanied him. Annie had found the brown tabby as an abandoned kitten in the backyard and brought her into the café. Ed had instantly bonded with the little scrap, and named her

AJ. Now the feline was all grown up and a loyal companion, although she was definitely independently minded.

"Now I have to call Father Mike." Zoe dug her phone out of her jeans' pocket and speed-dialed the priest. After a few minutes of conversation, she was all smiles.

"Father Mike says no problem and next week is good for him, too. He's busy this weekend with Ava's wedding."

"A lot of locals have been getting married recently," Lauren mused, sitting behind the counter. "Us, plus Brooke, and now Ava."

The door opened, and Ms. Tobin walked in.

"Brrt?" Annie trotted to greet her.

"Hello, girls," the tall, slim, middle-aged woman greeted them. Wearing a short-sleeved cream blouse and amber skirt, she looked pleased to see them.

"Hi, Ms. Tobin." Lauren slid off her stool and stood behind the espresso machine. "What can we get you?"

"A large latte, please, and one of your cupcakes, Lauren." She peered at the glass counter. "I see you have the blueberry creams. I'll have one of those."

"Coming right up." Lauren smiled at her. Ms. Tobin used to be their prickliest customer but she had mellowed since they'd saved her from a romance scam a while ago, and now they considered her a friend.

"Have you read the gossip column this week?" Zoe zipped over to the four-seater Annie had chosen.

"Yes." Ms. Tobin nodded. "I'm afraid I don't approve of these types of columns."

"Even when it seems to be good natured gossip?" Lauren asked, bringing the coffee and cupcake over to her.

"Even when," Ms. Tobin replied. "One wrong word and someone's feelings could get hurt."

"I guess I hadn't thought of it like that," Zoe said slowly. "It just seems like a lot of fun."

"Until it isn't," Ms. Tobin cautioned.

Their friend's warning made Lauren decide not to contribute any news herself – even nice gossip – to the column, unless it was about her new cupcake creation she still had to think up.

They moved on to more pleasant topics, such as inquiring after Ms. Tobin's cat.

"How is Miranda?" Lauren asked.

"She's such a sweet girl." Ms. Tobin's face lit up. "So good."

"Is she still sitting on your lap at night?" Zoe inquired.

"Yes." Ms. Tobin nodded. "But now I've taken your advice and make sure I have a drink by my side before I sit down, so I don't have to disturb her when I get thirsty."

"Brrt!" *Good idea!*

A while ago, the café had held a kitten adoption day to support the local shelter, and Annie had chosen an orange, brown, and white calico kitty for Ms. Tobin.

"And my childhood friend Miranda is coming to visit me again soon."

"That's great," Zoe enthused.

Calling her kitten the name of the childhood friend she'd lost touch with had inspired Ms. Tobin to track her down, with happy results. Now the two of them chatted regularly on the phone and adult Miranda had already visited her in Gold Leaf Valley.

More customers trickled in, and the girls made their apologies to Ms. Tobin. Annie seated each newcomer, then returned to her friend.

Just when most of the customers had departed including Ms. Tobin, Mitch strode in.

Lauren's heart fluttered at the sight of her husband. She didn't think she'd ever get tired of just *looking* at him. Tall, with a lean, muscular frame, he made her senses sing – and always would. His dark hair was cut short, and his brown eyes, straight nose, and firm chin added up to one good looking guy.

But it wasn't just his appearance that captured her heart – it was his appreciation of her as a person, and of her independence, as well.

"Hi." She greeted him with a big smile.

"Hi." He leaned over the counter and kissed her, not seeming to care there were a couple of customers seated nearby.

"Do you have to work late tonight?"

"No." His eyes crinkled at the corners. "I'm all yours."

"Good."

"I thought we could have dinner at the bistro."

"I'd like that." Lately they'd been staying in a lot, and having a date night would be fun. And, the bistro was where they'd held their wedding reception. Along with having great food, the rustic interior was welcoming and cozy.

"I'll book a table for seven," he proposed.

"Perfect."

She made him a large latte to go, and placed a blueberry cream into a paper bag for him.

"Thanks." He swiftly kissed her again. "See you tonight."

Lauren gazed after him, a dreamy smile on her face. Would married life always be like this? She certainly hoped so.

***

After the lunch rush, there was a distinct lull.

"Good," Zoe enthused. "Now we can zip over to the newspaper office."

"Brrt?" Annie was dozing in her pink cat basket, but opened one sleepy green eye.

"We're thinking of placing a small ad in the newspaper," Lauren told her fur baby.

"To drum up business," Zoe added. "It might give you lots more customers to seat."

"Brrt!" Annie woke properly and sat up straight.

"Do you want to go home while we're out, or do you want to mind the café?" Lauren asked. Ed had already left for the day, as he started early and finished early.

"Brrt." *Mind café.*

"We won't be long," Lauren promised. She'd feel happier if Annie was in the cottage, but she knew her fur baby thought of the coffee shop as "hers".

"I think I'll make myself a latte when we get back," Zoe said as Lauren locked up and waved goodbye to Annie. "Or maybe a cappuccino. Or a mocha. Or a—"

"We'd better hurry." Lauren set off briskly.

"You're right." Zoe caught up with her.

The newspaper office was around the corner, situated in a Victorian house that had been converted to office space. Since the town dated from the Northern California Gold Rush era, a lot of the dwellings were of a similar age, some kept nicely, and some a little run down.

The cream exterior, with peach gingerbread trim and neat green lawn, made it look like the small newspaper was doing well.

A bell tinkled above them as they entered the office.

A receptionist with neat copper-brown hair looked up from the computer screen. "Can I help you?" Her gaze was inquisitive.

"We'd like to place an ad in the next edition, if that's possible," Lauren began. "But we're not sure how much it will cost."

"Our rates are right here." The receptionist pointed to a laminated card facing them.

Lauren looked at the smallest ad size and was pleasantly surprised to see that she could afford it.

"I'll take this one." She pointed to the ad price.

"Fill in this form." The receptionist, whose name plate said Thelma, handed her a clipboard and a pen.

Zoe urged her over to the tiny waiting area, consisting of two hardbacked chairs, and leaned over as Lauren filled in the form.

"What are you going to say?"

Why hadn't she thought of writing up the ad first? She checked her watch.

"I don't want to take too long," she whispered back.

"I hear you. Well, you have to include Annie, and your cupcakes, and your coffee, and Ed's Danishes."

After a moment, Lauren came up with:

Our Norwegian Forest Cat will seat you.
Try our coffee, cupcakes, and delicious Danishes today!
The Norwegian Forest Cat Café, Gold Leaf Valley.

"That's good," Zoe approved. "Maybe you should be the writer instead of me!"

"I think I'll stick to these ads – if this one is successful."

"How can it not be? We've got everything anyone could possibly want when they walk into a café – including Annie."

She smiled in agreement, knowing that some of their customers only visited so they could spend time with her fur baby, although she thought by now they also enjoyed the coffee and sweet treats.

"Payment in advance," Thelma requested, when Lauren handed her the ad.

She reached into her purse for her wallet, and paid cash.

"The next edition comes out on Tuesday, doesn't it?" Zoe inquired.

"Yes. And your ad will be in it." Thelma glanced at the form. "Oh, you're that cute café with the cat."

"That's right. But I don't think I've seen you come in." Lauren crinkled her brow.

"I never have any time." The receptionist sounded disgruntled. "This job is only part-time and when I'm finished here for the day, I have a few clients I clean house for." She leaned forward. "I was hoping to get the gossip columnist job but my boss Phil gave it to his wife's friend instead." She shook her head in disgust. "I've written some of the stories in this paper, you know? I could do a great job writing gossip."

"Which stories have you written?" Zoe asked curiously.

"Last year's church bake sale, and when the new mechanic opened up shop here – small stories like that. But I'm ready for bigger ones too. I've worked here for years – I've got experience. You'd think that would count for something, but apparently not. You need to be a friend of your boss's wife to get anywhere in this place." She turned up her nose.

"I'm sorry," Lauren said awkwardly.

The receptionist shrugged. "I guess it is what it is. Anyway, I hope your ad does well. The handmade shop lady is already placing another ad for the next two weeks, and the mechanic has a weekly ad running because it's so successful."

"That reminds me." Zoe snapped her fingers. "I want to go to the mechanic's and check out that used car he has for sale."

"Good idea." Thelma nodded. "You don't want to miss out on something like that."

Lauren glanced at her watch. "We have to get back to the café."

"You're right," Zoe replied reluctantly.

"Thanks for—"

The inner office door creaked open and a man in his fifties poked his head out. He wore black rimmed glasses and his gray hair was rumpled, as if he'd run a hand through it several times.

"Thelma, have you finished that spreadsheet yet?" the man barked. He did a slight double take when he saw Lauren and Zoe, and lowered his tone. "Sorry, didn't realize you were here."

"We were just placing an ad," Zoe informed him.

"Good, good." He nodded. "I'm Phil, reporter, editor, and owner of the *Gazette*."

"I emailed it to you fifteen minutes ago," Thelma replied crisply.

"Did you?" He frowned. "I'll check my email again." He strode into the inner office. A couple of seconds later, he called out, "Got it!"

Thelma rolled her eyes. "You see what I've got to put up with? You'd think he'd give me the gossip columnist job after I've worked here for so long – as a sort of reward for putting up with him. He does this stuff all the time."

"How long *have* you been working here?" Zoe asked.

"Seven years." Thelma grimaced. "I might have to start looking for a job at another newspaper – if I can find one."

"What about Zeke's Ridge?" Lauren proposed. "Or do you cover that area, too?"

"They don't have their own newspaper," Thelma informed them. "It's a smaller town than Gold Leaf Valley and only twenty minutes away. We cover their news as well – if they have any." She chuckled, then brightened. "Hey, that's a good idea. I can cold call the businesses there and see if they want to put in an ad – I'll check with the boss and see if he'll pay me commission on any business I bring in from there."

"Awesome," Zoe enthused.

Thelma looked happier when they left, busy dialing a number on the landline.

They dashed back to the café. Annie was strolling around the room, as if checking for lost objects. She scampered over to them when they opened the oak and glass door.

"Brrt!"

Lauren picked her up and cuddled her close. "We weren't gone very long, were we?"

"Brrp." *Not really.*

"You're going to be in the ad, Annie," Zoe told her.

"Brrt!" Annie peeked happily at her, still snuggled in Lauren's arms.

"What's the time?" Zoe peered at Lauren's watch. "Only three – that's good. We can check out that used car at the mechanic's when we close today."

"I don't know if I'll have time. Mitch and I are going to the bistro for dinner tonight. He's booking a table for seven."

"And you'll be dolling yourself up." Zoe giggled. "Don't worry, I get it. Maybe Chris and I should have a date night soon. What about tomorrow after work? And then it's craft club the day after."

"That sounds good." Lauren smiled at her.

"Are you going to start your new blanket before Friday night?"

Lauren stared at her, realizing she hadn't picked up her knitting needles yet. Where were they? Somewhere in her closet?

"I might have to cast on at Mrs. Finch's," she admitted.

"That's probably the perfect place to do it. Mrs. Finch is an awesome knitter!"

CHAPTER 3

That evening, Lauren smiled at her husband across their cozy bistro table, covered with a white tablecloth. The restaurant's interior was rustic but elegant, and served some of her favorite food, including the desserts. Outside, fairy lights twinkled, although the sun hadn't quite descended yet. Located on the edge of town, it was one of their regular date night spots.

She wore her favorite plum wrap dress, which she knew Mitch liked, and the gold L necklace he'd given her when they'd dated.

Mitch looked handsome in a white dress shirt, and charcoal slacks and jacket.

"It's good to go out somewhere, just the two of us." He reached for her hand across the table.

"It is." Sometimes they double-dated with Zoe and Chris, often going over to their house for pizza or chili night, Annie included.

They'd already enjoyed their appetizer of stuffed mushrooms and were now waiting for their entrees – pan roasted salmon for Mitch, and pork with four varieties of apples for her.

She'd just finished telling Mitch about her plans to knit a lap blanket for the living room, when Zoe's comment about it doubling for a baby blanket flashed through her mind.

"Umm …" She glanced around the room, but the other few diners were at distant tables.

"What is it?" His brow creased.

"I was wondering …"

"What?" he urged, his fingers clasped around hers warmly and securely.

"When should we talk about having children?" she rushed out.

It was his turn to glance around the room.

"Right now, if you want to." His eyes crinkled at the corners.

"Well, I was thinking, we shouldn't leave it too late, but I don't think I'm ready to get pregnant right now. I'm enjoying it just being the two of us – three, with Annie."

"I feel the same." He squeezed her hand. "Just let me know when you think the time is right. I was thinking of two children – or even three."

"Three?" Her eyes widened and she leaned back a little in her chair.

"Two," he corrected hastily. "Or even one. You're the person who has to give birth."

Her heart fluttered at his thoughtfulness. "Thank you," she replied softly. "I think two would be the maximum for me – if we're lucky enough to be blessed twice."

He nodded, a tender smile on his face.

"But what about the café? I guess Zoe could be in charge while I'm looking after the baby, but who's going to make the cupcakes? Ed's specialty is his pastries, but I suppose I could ask him to try—"

"We'll work something out," he interrupted. "I guarantee it. Maybe I can get some paternity leave and help look after the baby when the time comes."

"That would be great." Relief swept through her.

They moved onto other topics as their entrees arrived – the food just as delicious as it had been on their wedding day.

Mitch's salmon was accompanied with a baked potato and steamed greens, while her pork was tender and the apple medley was sweet and fruity, perfectly complementing the meat.

Mitch told her about a case he was working on – there had been reports of a pickpocket in town.

"Be careful with your purse," he warned her, finishing his last bite of salmon.

"I will." She nodded. "I'll tell Zoe, too."

"Good. We don't have any leads at the moment, but it's not as if someone has reported a homeless stranger bumping up against people. It could be a tourist or someone from Sacramento trying their luck."

They finished their dinner with warm chocolate brownies and vanilla ice-cream. When they arrived home, Annie scampered from the living room to greet them.

"Did you have a good night too?" Lauren picked up the feline and held her. "What did you watch on TV?"

"Brrt!" *The princess movie!*

Lauren and Mitch walked into the living room, Mitch chuckling when he saw the end credits rolling on the screen.

"Of course." Lauren kissed the silver-gray tabby's forehead.

***

The next morning, Cee Cee, the gossip columnist, was their first customer.

"Hi." She swept into the café, wearing a gold toned shirt and cream skirt.

"Brrt!" Annie trotted over to her as she waited at the *Please Wait to be Seated* sign.

"What can we get you?" Lauren asked.

"I wish I could grab a table and sit with Annie, but I'm in a bit of a rush." She checked her watch. "Can I order some cupcakes for tomorrow and have them delivered to the newspaper office?"

Lauren and Zoe glanced at each other.

"We don't usually deliver during opening hours, but we can make an exception," Lauren told her. She hated losing any kind of business.

"Yeah, I can zip over with them," Zoe agreed.

"Wonderful." Cee Cee smiled at them. "It was Thelma's idea. Since you two placed an ad yesterday she's been complaining she never has time to try your cupcakes, so she came up with cupcake Friday."

"Which is tomorrow," Zoe observed.

"Exactly! And the boss agreed. So I'd like to order six, so we get two each."

"No problem." Lauren opened a drawer behind the counter and pulled out a notepad. She hadn't decided which flavors she was going to make for tomorrow yet. After a second, she suggested, "How about blueberry cream, triple chocolate ganache, and Norwegian apple?"

"Perfect!" Cee Cee clapped her hands. "Is payment on delivery okay? We're going to use the petty cash to pay for them."

"Okay." Lauren made a note on the order. "What time would you like them delivered?"

"Around ten?"

"That's doable." Zoe nodded. "We're usually not slammed by then."

"Brrt," Annie agreed.

"Have you two figured out who else I wrote about in this week's edition?" Cee Cee asked coyly.

"No," Lauren replied. She hadn't had a chance to read the rest of the gossip column yet.

"Let's see." Zoe rummaged behind the counter and pulled out the by now rumpled newspaper. "Lucky I kept it!"

"So many strawberries – who would have thought they'd attract so many people?"

"Ooh, I bet that's the owner of the grocery store!" Zoe sounded excited. "They had tons of strawberries last week. Lauren and I got some."

"You're right," Cee Cee replied. "Lauren, let me know when you have a new cupcake flavor and I'll put it in the column."

"Thanks." She'd have to get serious about thinking up something new.

Cee Cee ordered a large latte and an apricot Danish, telling them she was looking forward to their delivery the next day.

Lauren watched her walk out the door, Mitch's warning about pickpockets flashing through her mind. She tsked at herself.

"What?" Zoe prompted.

"Mitch told me last night there's a pickpocket in town, and to watch my purse. I should have told Cee Cee."

"Let's call the newspaper office." Zoe dug out her phone from her jeans' pocket. "We can leave a message with Thelma. You never know, it might make next week's gossip column!"

***

Lauren thought Mitch hadn't intended his pickpocket warning to be gossip fodder in the town's newspaper, but on the other hand, shouldn't forewarned be forearmed? But perhaps that wasn't the sort of gossip Cee Cee published and she wouldn't have to worry.

"Or maybe Thelma will pick up the story," she suggested to her cousin.

"Brrt!"

"Thelma didn't answer the phone." Zoe frowned at her screen. "I had to leave a voice mail."

The morning passed smoothly. When she wasn't busy, Lauren wracked her brain for new cupcake ideas, but nothing came to mind. Perhaps it would happen when she least expected it.

"Don't forget we're checking out that used car this afternoon," Zoe reminded her before she departed for her quick lunch break. They took turns, so someone would always be on duty in the café – apart from Annie.

"That's right. Have you told Chris about it?"

"Yes. And he's cool with the idea."

"Good." Lauren smiled.

Zoe zipped to the cottage to eat her lunch. When she returned, Lauren would take her break – with Annie. Her stomach rumbled at the thought of her meal – a turkey and cranberry panini she'd put aside that morning. Created out of bread she had delivered, she made up a small batch each morning when she was in the commercial kitchen baking the cupcakes.

Today, Zoe had brought her own can of tuna and a bag of salad leaves, saying she'd gotten used to being a little healthier with her eating.

"All yours," Zoe emerged from the private hallway that connected the café to the cottage.

"Thanks." For once, it was quiet during the lunch period.

Annie trotted by her side as they headed to the cottage.

"Would you like chicken in gravy?" Lauren took a small can out of the pantry and opened it, spooning brown lumps and gravy into the lilac bowl.

"Brrt!" Annie's pink tongue darted out and tasted it first, then she started eating enthusiastically.

Lauren sat down at the large pine table and unwrapped her panini. It had been good to have a date night with Mitch last evening, and she was glad they were on the same page when it came to starting a family – some time in the future.

Her thoughts turned to the small cupcake delivery for Cee Cee the next day, and then an idea flashed in her mind for a new cupcake. A Spring time cake, decorated with daisies.

"What do you think, Annie? A vanilla cupcake with lilac frosting, and daisies with white petals and yellow centers?"

"Brrt!" *Good idea.* She jumped up on the chair next to Lauren's and bunted her arm.

"I don't know if cranberry sauce is good for cats," she apologized. Better safe than sorry. She popped the last bite into her mouth and followed it with a glass of water. After writing down her cupcake idea, she headed back to the café with Annie.

Mrs. Finch came in that afternoon, and they updated her on Lauren's blanket project.

"I can't wait to see the yarn you've chosen." She sat at a small table Annie had chosen, sipping a cup of hot tea, her hand wobbling slightly.

"I'm looking forward to showing you," Lauren replied with a smile.

Zoe filled her in on their cupcake delivery to the newspaper office the next morning, and their upcoming visit to the car mechanic that day to check out the used car he had for sale.

"I wonder what color it is," Zoe said. "Maybe it's black, or white, or silver, or—"

"You'll find out this afternoon," Mrs. Finch teased gently.

"Brrt!"

***

They closed the café five minutes earlier than usual, as the last customer had departed a few minutes before.

Zoe zoomed around with the vacuum, while Lauren finished washing the dishes.

"All done!" Zoe surveyed the gleaming space. Annie prowled around the tables, but did not seem to find anything interesting.

"We're going to look at a car Zoe's interested in buying," Lauren told the feline. "Why don't you mind the cottage for me while we're gone? Mitch should be home around six tonight."

"Brrt." Annie pushed open the cat flap in the bottom of the door of the private hallway, and trotted toward the cottage kitchen door.

"Do you want something before we go?" Lauren asked, before she followed her fur baby.

"No, I'm good," Zoe replied. "The ad says the mechanic closes at six, so we have to skedaddle."

"Okay. I'll just give Annie her dinner."

Lauren spooned more chicken and gravy into the bowl, then said goodbye.

"I'll be back for dinner tonight."

"Brrp," she mumbled, busy investigating her meal.

Lauren smiled fondly at her, then locked up.

"Let's go." She joined her cousin in the café.

They hopped into Lauren's car, which was parked outside.

"I can't wait until I've got my own wheels." Zoe buckled her seatbelt. "Then I'll be able to drive *you* around."

"That would be good," Lauren replied with a smile.

"And I can drive Chris somewhere. Hmm. Maybe *I'll* take *him* to the bistro for dinner one night instead of him taking me. Ooh – I can make it a surprise!"

"I think he'd love that." She'd always thought that Zoe and Chris complemented each other. He was laid-back, easy-going, and a genuinely nice guy – a perfect foil for Zoe's impulsivity. And her cousin had a good heart and positive nature.

They drove to the mechanic's who was situated a few blocks away. There were a couple of older cars in the neat gravel yard, one black, and one a rusty shade of brown.

"I hope that brown sedan isn't for sale." Zoe sounded disappointed.

They walked up to the repair shop.

"Hello?" Zoe called.

Metal clattered nearby, and a man in his fifties stuck his head out from underneath a blue car. His dark hair was cut short, and there was a hint of balding around his crown. He wore a gray T-shirt stained with oil or grease, and faded blue jeans.

"Help you?" he asked pleasantly.

"Yes." Zoe beamed. "I saw your ad in the *Gold Leaf Valley Gazette* about a used car for sale."

"That's it over there." He pointed to the rusty brown vehicle.

"That one?" Zoe confirmed reluctantly.

"It's a great car for its age." He stood up and stuck out a slightly dirty hand, grease smudges on his fingers. He glanced at his hand and quickly wiped it with a clean cloth from his pocket. "I'm Gus. It's three thousand dollars, and only has fifty thousand miles on the clock."

"Why don't you take a proper look at it?" Lauren suggested. She hated seeing her cousin disappointed when she'd been so excited about coming here.

"Okay." Zoe zipped over to the brown car and peered through the sparkling driver's window. "It's got cup holders." She sounded more enthusiastic. "Ooh, a stick shift. I can drive that."

"The trunk has plenty of room for groceries, or whatever you want to use it for." He opened it up. Lauren was impressed with the space available.

"What about the back seats?" Zoe peeked through a rear window. "There's a patch on one."

"Yeah. Sorry about that. I had my wife fix it – she's good at stuff like that. It was either sew it up or replace the entire seat and that would have put up the price."

"What about the engine?" Lauren became interested.

"She's a good little thing," he told them. "Will take you anywhere."

"Will she take me to Sacramento?" Zoe asked.

"Of course."

"What about LA?"

"Yes."

"Hmm." Zoe walked around the vehicle, pondering.

"She's also got brand new tires."

"I don't know." Zoe turned to Lauren. "I was so excited about checking it out but now …" She spied the black car nearby. "What about that one?"

Gus chuckled. "That's mine."

"Oh." Zoe's expression fell.

"Have you had many inquiries about this car?" Lauren asked.

"A couple, but people seem to lose interest when they see the color." He sighed. "I was hoping to save costs by not repainting it, but it looks like I might have to. I hate to increase the price on it, but I'm not making much of a profit if I sell it at the current price as is."

"Why *are* you selling it?" Zoe inquired.

"I picked it up cheap from a newspaper ad, but now I can see why." He grimaced. "I don't usually make such a mistake, but I guess ladies are pickier about colors than men, and the one guy who came to look at it said it wasn't sporty enough." He shook his head. "What do you expect for three grand?

"I forgot to tell you I'm also guaranteeing this car is mechanically sound for a full two years. If you have any problems during that period– not that you should – bring it back and I'll fix whatever's wrong on the house."

"That sounds good," Lauren replied.

Zoe circled the car once again. "I just don't know." She sighed.

"What if you painted it red, or another color?" Lauren suggested to Gus.

"Ooh!" Zoe's eyes widened. "Yeah, I can just see myself driving along in a red car." She pulled open the driver's door. "Can I test out the horn?"

A loud beep startled Lauren.

"Great horn." Zoe patted the dashboard.

Gus studied the two of them.

"How about I paint it red, no obligation, and if you want to buy it then, I'll charge you the paint job at cost. And if you still don't want it, no problem."

"What sort of red?" Zoe wanted to know. "Not a pink red. It has to be a red red." She paused. "A Zoe red!"

Lauren stifled a giggle. She caught Gus's eye. "Do you have a color chart we could look at?"

"Sure." He sounded relieved.

"If this car is a Zoe red, I can definitely see myself driving it," Zoe enthused, as they followed him into the little office.

"What about a test drive?" Lauren suddenly asked.

"No problem. Before or after the paint job?" Gus replied.

"Before. No, after. No—"

"Before," Lauren decided. She turned to her cousin. "If you don't like the way the car handles, then there's no point Gus painting it Zoe red."

"True." Zoe sobered.

"Okay. Let's all go for a test drive." He led them back to the car.

"My husband brought his car in to get serviced," Lauren told him. "Mitch Denman."

"The police detective." He nodded. "Nice guy."

"Thanks." She checked her watch. Mitch was probably home by now.

"Why don't we go around the block a few times?" Gus suggested.

Zoe started the engine. It purred. A smile lit her face.

"See? Told you it was a good engine."

"Mm." Zoe drove out of the yard and down the street.

Lauren had chosen to sit in the back, with the mechanic next to her cousin. She wriggled against the upholstery. Pretty comfy.

Zoe shifted gears easily, tooting the horn when there weren't any other cars.

"I like this horn." She grinned.

"This car doesn't use a lot of gas, either," the mechanic pointed out.

If Lauren hadn't been happy with her current car, she would have been tempted to purchase this one.

Zoe zoomed them back to the mechanic's. "Can we look at the color chart now?"

"No problem."

He ushered them into the tiny room, sporting a battered desk and an old ergonomic chair. Pulling a paint chart off the desk, he pointed to it. "I can paint it any of these shades using a metallic paint for an extra three-hundred-and-forty dollars. That's cost price."

Lauren nodded. It sounded reasonable to her.

"Hmm." Zoe's finger hovered over one red shade, and then another. "This red – no, this red – no, *this* red!" Her finger stabbed a true, bright red.

"Okay." He nodded. "I'll start painting it tonight."

"That fast?" Zoe sounded delighted.

"Why not?" He shrugged. "I'll call my wife and tell her I'll be home late."

"Is that her?" Lauren gestured to a photo on the desk featuring a woman who looked around the same age as Gus, her arm wrapped around a teen boy.

"Yeah." He nodded. "And that's Brian, our foster son."

"Will you call me when the car is ready for me to look at again?" Zoe dug out her phone. "I'll give you my number."

He wrote it down on a notepad.

"Wait until I tell Cee Cee tomorrow!" Zoe grinned.

"Cee Cee?"

"The gossip columnist lady. You know, from the *Gold Leaf Valley Gazette*," Zoe answered. "She recommended you after I mentioned I'd seen your ad in the newspaper about the car."

"They started the column about six weeks ago," Lauren added.

"Oh, that lady." Gus nodded. "I've seen her around. I usually deal with Thelma when I call or visit the office to place my ad."

"Do you read the column?" Zoe asked. "We do. It's a lot of fun. Did you know Ava is getting married and Father Mike is officiating?"

"No." He looked mystified. "I don't think I know who Ava is."

"Oh." Zoe sounded disappointed.

"Thank you for showing us the car," Lauren said. "We'd better get going."

"I can't wait to see it painted *my* red!" Zoe waved goodbye, and hopped into Lauren's white compact.

"I'll have to bring Chris to see Zoe Two." Her eyes lit up.

"Zoe Two?" Lauren drove down the street.

"If it's going to be Zoe red, then it's definitely Zoe Two." She giggled. "That was a great idea, Lauren, asking Gus to paint it red. I don't even mind the stitched-up back seat now. I think it gives her character."

Zoe chattered all the way back to her rental about the new car. Lauren didn't need to do much apart from nod and smile at the appropriate times.

"And I have just enough saved up to pay for it, including the new paint job," she enthused as Lauren pulled up outside her rental, a slightly shabby Victorian with fading green paint. The surrounding cottages looked more spruced up.

"That's great," Lauren replied. She meant it.

"Isn't it?" Zoe grinned. "Wait until I tell Chris all about it!"

"You can tell Mrs. Finch tomorrow night as well."

"Definitely!"

CHAPTER 4

"Hi, Ed." Lauren stepped into the café kitchen the next morning.

"What's up?" Ed, her pastry chef, with monster rolling pins for arms, looked up from the dough he was patting into shape. His shaggy auburn hair looked like it needed a trim.

She explained how they had a small delivery to complete that morning.

"I was thinking I could dash out with Zoe, as I've come up with a new cupcake idea. Cee Cee asked me to let her know so she can put it in the gossip column. I might be able to make the deadline for next week."

"Sure, no problem." He smiled briefly.

"Thanks. We'll leave when there aren't any customers – hopefully around ten."

"If there are any, I'll take care of them," he promised. "I know Annie will help as well."

"She will." Lauren smiled.

"Well?" Zoe asked, when she returned to the counter.

"Ed will look after things while we're gone, but I only want the delivery to take a few minutes."

"No worries."

Lauren boxed up the order and put it to one side.

"It's a shame Cee Cee didn't want them delivered now." Zoe peeked at Lauren's watch. "We could have zipped over there and back in five minutes and have four minutes to spare before we open."

"True." Lauren nodded.

Only a couple of customers entered before ten. Once Annie seated them and they were enjoying their treats, Lauren hurried into the kitchen.

"We're going to the newspaper office now, Ed."

"No problem." He looked up from the second batch of apricot Danishes he was making. "I'll keep an ear out."

"I'm sure Annie will let you know if she needs help."

"Yep." He grinned.

Lauren said goodbye to her fur baby, explaining the situation, then she and Zoe left the café.

Striding briskly past quaint little shops open for business, she said hello to a couple of customers, saying they had a delivery to make, but would be back in the café shortly.

"See? I told you it wouldn't take long." Zoe pointed to Lauren's watch when they reached the cream and peach Victorian.

"You're right."

Zoe pushed open the white wooden door to the office as Lauren held the box of cupcakes.

"Hello?" Zoe called out.

They entered the reception area, but Thelma was not behind her desk.

"Maybe she stepped out for a moment," Lauren suggested.

"But it's cupcake Friday." Zoe frowned. "I thought she'd be here."

"So did I." And, she reminded herself, it was cash on delivery. Where was everyone?

"Maybe her boss Phil is in his office," Zoe suggested.

Lauren placed the box of treats on the reception desk and eyed the closed inner door.

"Should we knock?"

"Yes." Zoe rounded the reception desk and rapped on the door. It swung inward. "Hello? Phil? We've brought cupcakes for you."

The inner – and outer – office was silent, apart from Lauren's rapid heartbeat. She suddenly had a sinking feeling.

"Are you in there?" Zoe stepped forward.

"Zoe—" Lauren's warning was cut off as her cousin gasped.

Rushing to her side, she steeled herself for whatever she was about to find.

She hadn't expected to glimpse Cee Cee lying dead on the floor – strangled!

CHAPTER 5

A copy of last week's *Gold Leaf Valley Gazette* was placed on Cee Cee's chest.

"That looks like the lamp cord from the desk light." Zoe pointed with a shaking finger at the black cord wrapped around the gossip columnist's neck.

"I guess we'd better check for a pulse." Her voice wobbled.

"Chris showed me how, and I don't have a compact with me – do you?" Zoe turned to her.

"No." She shook her head.

Together, they carefully approached Cee Cee's body. Zoe touched her fingers to the woman's wrist. After a moment, she said, "No pulse."

Lauren glanced around the room, but other than poor Cee Cee, everything else looked to be in order – apart from the desk lamp, lying next to Cee Cee's body.

"I'd better call Mitch." Lauren stepped toward the door. Zoe followed.

"I wonder where Thelma and Phil are." Zoe frowned.

Lauren pulled her phone out of her purse and speed-dialed her husband. Luckily, he answered, otherwise she'd have to call emergency services directly.

He promised to be there in a couple of minutes.

Footsteps sounded in the suddenly somber air.

"Is Mitch here already?" Zoe asked. "That was quick."

"Thelma?" A well-dressed man in his thirties came into the reception area. He wore a smart white shirt, dark slacks, and a light-weight blazer. His blond hair was brushed back from his forehead. "Cee Cee?" He did a double-take when he saw them.

"Who are you?" Zoe asked.

"I could say the same." His gaze flickered from the two of them to the inner office door, which they'd left open. "Where's Thelma or Cee Cee? Or Phil?"

"We don't know where Thelma or Phil are," Lauren replied, trying to place the stranger. She couldn't remember seeing him before. She exchanged a glance with Zoe, who also seemed mystified.

"What about Cee Cee?" he persisted.

"I'm afraid she can't help you right now," Lauren told him.

"Yeah." Zoe nodded. "She can't."

"Why not? I had a piece of gossip for her column, and she also talked me into placing an ad for next week. I'm not late for the deadline, am I?"

"I have no idea," Lauren replied, feeling awkward. All she wanted to do was sit down. Then speak to Mitch. Then return to the café and cuddle Annie for a few minutes. And make herself a mocha.

"So, who are you?" Zoe persisted.

"I'm Bryce," he admitted. "I've just joined the local real estate agency."

"That must be why we don't have a clue who you are." Zoe relaxed slightly.

"I think we should all step outside," Lauren said. "The police will be arriving any minute."

"The police?" His gaze sharpened. "What did you do?"

"What did *we* do?" Zoe drew in a deep breath.

Mitch strode into the room. Relief flowed through her.

"Are you okay?" He cupped her shoulders and looked at her in concern.

"I am now." She summoned a smile.

"Hey, what's going on?" Bryce demanded.

A uniformed office joined them and escorted Bryce outside.

"We have no idea who that guy is," Zoe told Mitch, "apart from being a real estate agent called Bryce. He just appeared out of nowhere."

"She's right," Lauren said. She quickly told him how they'd discovered Cee Cee's body.

"And we don't know where Thelma or Phil are," she finished.

"Stay here." Mitch pulled on latex gloves and entered the inner office. When he returned, he made a phone call.

"Why are the police here?" Thelma ran into the small waiting area. "Lauren? Zoe? What are you doing here?"

"We were delivering your cupcakes," Lauren managed.

"For cupcake Friday," Zoe reminded her.

"Detective Denman?" Phil had followed Thelma, a concerned look on his face. "What's going on?"

"Cee Cee has been murdered," Mitch informed them.

"What?" Thelma paled, and clasped a hand to her chest.

"Are you sure?" Phil frowned. "Where? When? How?"

"I'll take your statement in a minute, including your movements this morning," Mitch replied firmly. "Right now, Lauren and Zoe need to return to the café."

He escorted them out of the building, then turned to Lauren. "Are you sure you're going to be okay?"

"I'll be fine," she managed to reassure him.

"I'll probably have to work late tonight," he warned, "but I'll call you as soon as I finish here."

"Okay." She managed a smile.

They walked back to the café.

"Who would want to kill Cee Cee?" She couldn't get the horrific last image of the gossip columnist out of her head.

"I don't know. She seemed like a nice lady," Zoe replied. She suddenly stopped in her tracks. "Hey, what if Ms. Tobin was right? *One wrong word and someone's feelings could get hurt.*"

"Except this time, feelings weren't the only things involved."

***

As soon as they arrived at the café, Lauren scooped Annie in her arms.

"Brrt." The silver-gray tabby snuggled into Lauren's chest, as Lauren delicately told her what happened.

"I'll fill Ed in." Zoe swung through the kitchen doors. Lauren could hear the sound of their voices, then Zoe emerged.

"Ed wants to know if there's anything he can do for us."

"No." Lauren shook her head. "But it's a kind thought."

"That's what I said." Zoe nodded.

Ed stuck his head through the swinging doors. "Do you want to take the rest of the day off?" he asked in concern.

Lauren was tempted for a moment, then saw all the cupcakes in the glass cases, as well as Ed's delicious pastries waiting for customers. She knew some of their regulars depended on their interactions and chats with Annie to brighten their day.

"No, I think we should keep trading as usual," she replied. Turning to Zoe, she asked, "Is that okay with you?"

"Definitely." Zoe nodded. "I think it's best we take our mind off things by working."

"No worries." Ed returned to his pastry making.

Martha barreled into the café, pushing her rolling walker at a fast clip. Her pink capris and matching T-shirt looked cool and comfy, and complimented her curly gray hair.

"Do you know what's going on at the newspaper office?" she asked breathlessly.

"Brrt!" Annie wriggled in Lauren's arms.

She placed her fur baby gently onto the black vinyl padded seat of Martha's walker.

"Yes," she replied glumly.

"We'll tell you all about it," Zoe said.

"Goody."

"It won't be goody," Lauren warned.

"Oh." Martha's face fell. "Someone didn't die, did they?"

"Yes." Zoe nodded.

"Oh, no."

Annie directed Martha in the direction of a four-seater in a series of subdued brrts and brrps. Lauren and Zoe followed.

"Fill me in," Martha urged.

"What can I get you?" Lauren asked.

"I definitely need something, too," Zoe said. Her eyes widened. "What if we make you a special drink? I've just thought of something."

"Better than hot chocolate with lots of marshmallows?" Martha asked. "Better than Martha's marshmallow latte?"

"I think it might be." Zoe nodded.

"Then count me in!"

"I'll make one for you too, Lauren. But I might need your help. You're better at steaming milk than I am."

"You're pretty good," Lauren replied, but she followed her cousin to the espresso machine.

"I'm thinking a latte, with pumpkin spice mixed into the espresso, and then marshmallows as well."

Lauren stared at her, running the combination through her mind.

"That could work," she said slowly.

"I think so, too." Zoe smiled briefly. "After all, most people love Martha's marshmallow latte."

Lauren suddenly thought of something. "What about adding hot chocolate powder to it as well?"

"And turn it into a pumpkin spice marshmallow mocha?" Zoe's brown eyes lit up. "Genius!"

"We won't know until we've tasted it," Lauren warned.

"Let's do it!"

Lauren pulled the espresso shot and steamed the milk, while Zoe fetched the pumpkin spice and got the hot chocolate powder and marshmallows ready.

She added the spice to the espresso, along with the chocolate powder. Pouring the milk foam into the cup, she added some mini marshmallows and gently stirred them through.

"It looks great, but I think it needs a little extra something." Zoe sprinkled hot chocolate powder on top. "There."

"Let's see what it tastes like." Lauren eyed the concoction, the aroma of the coffee and spices stirring her senses. She took a sip, and then another. "It works." She smiled at her cousin.

"Awesome! You have that one and I'll make one for me and Martha."

Lauren perched on the stool, taking comfort from her pumpkin spiced beverage while Zoe set to work.

"How's it coming?" Martha called from her table.

"Brrt?" Annie sat next to her friend.

"It's delicious," Lauren replied.

"Yours will be ready in a jiff," Zoe sang out. "We had to make a prototype first."

"Goody."

After Zoe made the drinks, they rejoined Martha and Annie.

"What's in it?" Martha's eyes widened as she stared at her mug, the sprinkle of chocolate powder on top of the micro foam tempting one to taste it immediately.

Lauren ran through the ingredients. "I've drunk half of mine already," she admitted.

"Take a sip," Zoe urged. "If you don't like it, we'll make you something else."

"Can't argue with that." Martha picked up the mug. After a moment, a big smile creased her face. "I don't like it – I *love* it!"

"Even better than Martha's marshmallow latte?" Zoe asked hopefully.

"Even better." Martha took a big sip with evident enjoyment.

"Let's write it up and make a special of it," Lauren suggested to Zoe.

"Good idea. As soon as I've finished mine!"

They all laughed, then sobered as they filled in Martha on finding Cee Cee's body.

"But I love reading her column," Martha mourned. "I met Cee Cee once at the senior center. She introduced herself and said she was looking for gossip."

"Did you have any for her?" Lauren asked curiously.

"A couple of tidbits, but she said she already knew about it, and had mentioned both items in her column."

"Really?" Zoe asked.

"I read her column every week and I didn't know what she printed was the same as what I told her." Martha frowned. "Maybe she wrote it in some kind of code so nobody would get upset about it."

"But we all knew who she referred to when she put in that wedding bells snippet about Father Mike marrying off Ava," Lauren mused.

"True." Martha nodded. "Maybe she put simple stuff like that in everyday language and put the real juicy stuff in some sort of code."

Zoe jumped up and fetched the newspaper. "Let's see." She thumbed through the pages, making a rustling noise. "Here's her column from last week. The wedding bells one, and … what about this one? *A little birdie told me echoed whispers often come to a dead end.*"

"I haven't read that one." Lauren's eyes widened. "But—"

"It sounds like Cee Cee foretold her own death," Zoe finished.

CHAPTER 6

After Martha finished an apricot Danish as well as a second pumpkin spice marshmallow mocha, she waved goodbye.

Lauren's phone buzzed. Mitch. She assured him she was okay, and reminded him it was craft club that night.

"I'll save some cupcakes for you and leave them in our kitchen," she promised before ending the call.

"Has Mitch got any news?" Zoe finished writing up the new drink on the miniature chalkboard and placed it near the register.

"No. But he'll be working late."

"And we can talk everything over with Mrs. Finch tonight."

"Brrt!"

***

That evening, Lauren left a box of three cupcakes on the table for Mitch

– blueberry cream, triple chocolate ganache, and Norwegian apple.

She and Zoe had a quick dinner together – left over beef stew – and got ready for craft club.

"Have you got your knitting?" Zoe called out.

"No." Lauren dashed to her bedroom and rooted through the closet. Tucked away were her needles. Phew. She grabbed the bag of yarn she'd bought the other day and stashed both items in a tote bag. "Now I have." She emerged from the bedroom.

"Brrt," Annie said in approval.

"What about you?" Lauren asked her cousin. "I'd love to read your script one day – when it's ready," she added, noticing a look of slight panic on Zoe's face.

"I'd love for you to read it." Zoe nodded. "And I love talking about it in general terms, but what if it's not ready to give to someone else to read? What if it's *never* ready?"

Lauren looked at her in surprise. It wasn't like Zoe to have a crisis of confidence.

"I'm sure you'll know the exact time when it *is* ready," she assured her. "You've come up with some great ideas."

"Thanks." Zoe brightened. "And I'm looking forward to my playdate next week with Annie, Mrs. Snuggle, and AJ."

"Brrt!" *Me too!*

They drove to Mrs. Finch's house, just a block away. Sometimes they walked, but after the shock of finding Cee Cee that morning, and Lauren carrying her tote bag with her new knitting project, she felt like being lazy.

"Maybe I can drive us to craft club next week." Zoe's eyes lit up. "If my new car is ready by then."

"Brrt!" Annie said encouragingly.

"Thanks." Zoe twisted in the passenger seat to beam at the feline.

They pulled up outside their friend's sweet Victorian house. It was painted cream, and had a neat green lawn with orange Californian poppies giving it a cheerful touch in the early evening sunshine.

"Come in, come in," Mrs. Finch urged when she opened the front door, a smile on her face. Tonight she wore a green skirt and matching blouse, her hair piled up a touch untidily in her usual bun.

"We've got a lot to tell you," Zoe said, as they passed through the lilac painted hall and into the beige and fawn living room.

"Sit down," Mrs. Finch urged, taking her usual armchair.

The trio shared the fawn sofa, then Annie hopped down and jumped up onto the arm of Mrs. Finch's chair. Their friend obliged by stroking her gently.

"Where do we start?" Zoe glanced at Lauren.

"What about your projects?" Mrs. Finch eyed Lauren's tote bag.

"Oh, yes." Lauren pulled out the balls of blue and cream yarn as well as the knitting needles. "I'd like to make a lap blanket."

"She thinks her pink living room might be too girly for Mitch." Zoe giggled.

"They look like lovely colors." Mrs. Finch duly admired the yarn. "What sort of stitch were you thinking of using?"

Lauren cast her a panicked look. She could only do the basics – garter, purl, and stockinette.

"Stockinette stitch," she said after a moment. "Although I'm not great at changing colors."

"That will come with practice," Mrs. Finch assured her. "You've made some lovely things already, such as your hat and a few scarves."

"I love the scarf you knitted me last year," Zoe enthused.

"Thanks." Lauren smiled.

"Why don't you cast on, and Zoe can update me on her screenplay?" their friend suggested.

Lauren nodded, and made a loop in the blue yarn, thrust a needle through it, and then started clacking away. She wasn't great at casting on either, although she could do it. And she knew if she got stuck, Mrs. Finch would help her.

Zoe launched into the upcoming playdate with Annie, Mrs. Snuggle, and AJ.

"But," she paused dramatically, "we have even more news! I checked out a car for sale at the local mechanic's – you know, Gus – and I love it! Well, I will once it's painted Zoe red!"

"Zoe red?' Mrs. Finch's eyes widened. "You must tell me all about that."

Zoe did so, Lauren listening with a little smile on her face. If only they hadn't found Cee Cee that morning, this evening would be very pleasant. But the topic of Cee Cee's death was in the back of her mind, and she was sure it was in the back of her cousin's, as well.

When Zoe finished telling Mrs. Finch about Zoe Two, she sobered. "And then –" she hesitated.

"Oh, no." Mrs. Finch picked up on the suddenly somber mood. "Did something else happen?"

"Brrt," Annie replied, bunting Mrs. Finch's hand for another gentle stroke.

"I'm afraid," Lauren spoke, "we discovered Cee Cee this morning."

"Strangled."

CHAPTER 7

Mrs. Finch sank back in her chair, visibly shocked.

"Oh, no."

"We don't have to talk about it if you'd rather not," Lauren said delicately.

"I suppose I'll hear it from someone at some time," Mrs. Finch replied. "I think it's best if you two tell me. Three." She glanced at Annie.

"Annie wasn't there, thank goodness," Lauren said. "She was minding the café."

Zoe filled her in, not going into detail about the way Cee Cee looked, which Lauren appreciated.

"But we don't know who this real estate guy Bryce is," she finished. "I've never seen him before."

"Hmm." Mrs. Finch closed her eyes for a second. "I can't say I've heard of him, either. Or why the agency needs another person working for them. It's quite small."

"Maybe they're expanding?" Lauren suggested.

"Or someone's retiring. Or got fired!" Zoe turned to her. "We'll have to check it out."

"I'm sure Mitch will," she replied.

"Maybe he won't have time. We could do it for him."

"We'll see," Lauren said.

"Brrt!" *Yes!*

"Did you get paid for the cupcakes, Lauren?" Mrs. Finch opened her eyes.

"No," she admitted. "And I don't feel comfortable pursuing it after what happened to Cee Cee."

"Thelma and Phil probably needed those cupcakes today," Zoe remarked. "Therapy."

"I do hope they'll be okay," Mrs. Finch remarked. "I wonder why Thelma wasn't in the office when you arrived with their treats? Didn't Zoe say cupcake Friday was Thelma's idea?"

"That's what Cee Cee told us when she came into the café yesterday to order them," Lauren replied.

"Yeah, it was strange there was no one in the office when we got there," Zoe added.

"Brrt!"

"I'm sure Mitch will figure it out – or you two – three –will." Mrs. Finch gave them a fond smile. "But you must be careful. I don't want anything happening to you."

"Me neither." Lauren clacked her knitting needles together. Oops. She'd just made a hole. She didn't think she would ever reach the stage where she would *not* make a hole in a project.

"I wonder what will happen to Cee Cee's gossip column now?" Zoe tapped her cheek. "Will they abandon it, or hire someone else to do it?"

"Thelma might be interested," Lauren said.

"You're right!" Zoe turned to her. "Didn't she say the other day that she was annoyed that her boss Phil hired Cee Cee, who was a friend of his wife's, when Thelma had been working there for years and had written some of the smaller stories?"

"We should inform Mitch, in case Thelma hasn't thought of telling him that," Lauren said.

"Brrt!"

***

By the time the evening drew to a close, Lauren had knitted three rows of her blanket, and they made Mrs. Finch a little latte, using her capsule machine. They'd also told her about the pickpocket in town, warning her to be careful.

"We'll visit you on Sunday or Monday," Zoe promised.

"I'll look forward to it." Mrs. Finch beamed, waving goodbye to them.

Zoe buckled her seatbelt in the car and turned on her phone.

"I'm going to make a list. Find out who this real estate guy is, why Thelma wasn't there when we delivered the cupcakes, and discover when Zoe Two will be ready to show Chris."

"I thought you'd practically made up your mind to buy it." Lauren drove through the dark, quiet streets until they reached Zoe's house.

"I have," Zoe admitted. "But it will still be fun to show Chris first. He's off on Monday, so I'll call Gus and check if it's okay to stop by to see the paint job."

"That sounds like a good idea."

***

The next morning, Hans entered the café just after they opened.

"Brrt!" Annie scampered to greet him.

"Hello, Lauren, and Zoe." The dapper German's faded blue eyes twinkled. "Hello, *Liebchen*." He glanced down at Annie.

"Brrt." *Hello.* She slowly led him to a four-seater near the counter, as if sensing he couldn't walk quickly.

"What can we get you?" Lauren and Zoe approached the duo. Usually, customers came to the counter to place their order, but they relaxed this rule for the elderly, infirm, and just plain harried. They also relaxed it for their regular customers as well, particularly Annie's – and their – favorites when business was slow.

"My usual cappuccino please," Hans replied. "And—"

"You don't want to try our new pumpkin spice marshmallow mocha?" Zoe asked.

"It's delicious," Lauren admitted, "I ended up having two yesterday."

"Then I must try it." He smiled. "And one of your cupcakes, please, Lauren."

"I have super vanilla, red velvet, and lavender today."

"A lavender, I think."

Since Ed didn't work on Saturdays, the cupcakes were the only sweet offerings that morning.

"We can ask Hans if he knows the new real estate guy," Zoe whispered to her as she steamed the milk.

"Good idea."

Zoe plated the treat while Lauren made the pumpkin spice beverage. She glanced over at Hans's table – Annie chattered to him in a series of brrts and brrps, and he seemed to be listening intently.

"If you don't like this latte, I'll make whatever you'd like," Lauren promised. She placed the steaming mug in front of him, the chocolate powder sprinkled on the top promising a delicious discovery.

"If you created it, I'm sure I will like it," Hans replied, lifting the mug to his lips.

They watched expectantly as he took his first sip.

"Ahh. That is good … in an unusual way." He sounded a little surprised – but delighted. "What have you been doing this week? I visited my daughter for a couple of days in Sacramento but the coffee there is not as good as yours."

"Thank you." Lauren smiled at one of her favorite people.

"Did you hear about Cee Cee, the gossip columnist?" Zoe leaned toward him.

"No." Hans frowned. "What has happened?"

"She was killed." Zoe filled him in.

Since Hans was their only customer right now, they sat down at the table.

"Ach, that is terrible." He shook his head. "I must admit I read the gossip, but sometimes I could not work out who she was talking about."

"What about the wedding bells and Father Mike?" Zoe asked. "We guessed who that was."

"Yes, Ava." Hans nodded.

"What about this one?" Lauren grabbed the newspaper from behind the counter. *"A little birdie told me echoed whispers often come to a dead end."*

"I saw that, but I did not know what it meant," he admitted.

"Me neither." Zoe frowned. "Hey, have you heard about a new real estate guy in town?"

"Yes, I have." Hans nodded. "I was walking past there the other day on the way to the grocery store, when I saw a sign in the window, welcoming their new agent. The other man who was there has gone to LA."

"We'll have to check it out," Zoe told Lauren and Annie.

"Or Mitch can," Lauren replied.

"If he has time." Zoe winked.

More customers came in, and they regretfully said goodbye to Hans. Annie seated the newcomers, then returned to him, until he finished his treats and said goodbye to all of them.

"Your pumpkin spice marshmallow mocha is delicious." Hans beamed as he paid his bill. "Thank you."

"Anytime." Lauren smiled.

"Definitely!" Zoe added.

***

The rest of the morning was busy, so by the time they closed at lunch, Lauren needed a break.

"Phew!" Zoe beat her to it, and sank onto a stool.

"That's what I was about to say," Lauren teased, sitting on the other stool and dangling her sneaker-clad feet.

"Brrt?"

Annie looked fresh and ready to play for the rest of the day.

"We have to clean up first before we can go home," Lauren reminded her.

"And then we can have fun!" Zoe's eyes sparkled.

"What are you going to do?" Lauren asked curiously.

Zoe's face fell. "Some housework. I've been busy working on my script, so I haven't done as much lately as I should. And I have two loads of laundry to do. Chris has been taking some extra shifts to save up for our honeymoon."

Zoe and Chris had gotten married unexpectedly, and hadn't gone anywhere for their honeymoon. Lauren and Mitch had visited Hawaii, with Zoe and Chris looking after Annie.

"Let me know when you want to take some time off."

"I will." Zoe smiled. "I can't decide where we should go. Hawaii like you, or the Caribbean like Brooke, or on a cruise, or—"

"Has Chris suggested anywhere?" she asked.

"Not really. I think he's more focused on getting the money together first, and then we can decide." A thought seemed to strike her. "Do you think I should put off buying Zoe Two and put the money toward our honeymoon?"

"Have you talked it over with Chris?"

"No," she admitted. "I was thrilled about her being painted red, and when I told Chris he seemed excited for me, but now ..."

Lauren stared at her cousin. It wasn't like her to be having second thoughts about something she'd set her heart on.

"I think you need your own car, don't you?"

Zoe nodded.

"Brrt," Annie agreed.

"So why don't you talk it over with Chris? How much money have you two got saved for your honeymoon, anyway? It might nearly be enough."

"You're right." Zoe's face cleared. "I know! I could make another batch of pottery mugs to make a little extra."

"I would love that, and so would our customers."

Zoe had recently explored pottery, with great results. She'd made several batches of mugs for the café and their customers, painting Annie in a variety of poses. Lauren paid for the materials and gave Zoe commission.

"I'll start thinking of a new idea for the mugs." Zoe looked happier.

They made arrangements to go to church the next day.

"And we could visit Mrs. Finch afterward, if you and Mitch aren't busy," Zoe suggested.

"I think Annie would like that."

"Brrt!"

Lauren and Annie returned to the cottage. Zoe wasn't the only one who had housework to do. She hoped she and Mitch could have a cozy dinner that evening, just the two of them – three, including Annie.

After a quick lunch, Lauren plugged in the vacuum. Annie trotted to the living room and hopped on the sofa, watching her wield it around the room. Perhaps she should buy one of those robot vacuums? What would Annie think? The thought made her giggle, wondering if Annie would chase it around the house.

When Mitch came home from the station, she looked at him in concern.

"Are you okay?" There were shadows under his eyes.

"I'm fine." He smiled and kissed her tenderly. "Nothing a night home with you won't fix."

"Brrt?"

"And you, Annie." He laughed and looked at the silver-gray tabby. "What have you been up to today?"

Annie chattered away to him in a series of brrts and brrps as Lauren fixed him a latte on her home espresso machine. She marveled at the way he related to Annie now, because when she'd met him, he hadn't been used to cats at all. But now the two of them got along like the good friends they were.

"How's the case coming along?" Lauren asked, sitting next to him at the kitchen table. Annie perched on the chair next to Lauren's and looked at him intently.

"The boss has put me in charge of Cee Cee's murder," he said in satisfaction after taking a healthy sip. "But Castern's nose is out of joint, because he's been tasked with the pickpocket case."

"Good." Lauren nodded.

Detective Castern was a thorn in Mitch's side. The older detective sometimes used slipshod methods to catch criminals and had ended up apprehending the wrong person – more than once.

"He grumbled all yesterday about it. I was glad he wasn't in the office today."

"At craft club last night we warned Mrs. Finch about the pickpocket."

"Hopefully Castern will catch him in the act. His idea is to walk around town like an unsuspecting citizen to seem like an easy mark."

"Did he do that today?" Lauren asked. She didn't remember seeing the detective walk past the café, but that didn't mean anything. They'd been busy with customers that morning.

"No. He said none of the victim reports mentioned being targeted on the weekend, so he's playing golf instead."

"And your boss allowed him?"

Mitch shrugged. "He's entitled to days off, and the boss looked at the reports. Castern was right."

"I hope he does nab this pickpocket. And I know you'll catch Cee Cee's killer."

"I hope to." He nodded and finished his latte. "That hit the spot. Thanks." He leaned back in his chair and stretched. "Do you want to go out for dinner tonight or stay in?"

"Stay in," she said without hesitation. "I can cook us something."

"I'd love that, but I was actually thinking we could order a pizza if you didn't want to eat out."

"I'd love that too." Lauren smiled.

When the pizza arrived, Annie had already finished her dinner of beef and liver and joined them at the kitchen table.

Mitch had ordered an extra large half and half. One side was a Lauren special consisting of Canadian bacon, mushroom, and sundried tomato, and the other side was a Zoe special of pepperoni and sausage.

"I interviewed Thelma and Phil at the newspaper office yesterday," he told her. She'd barely seen him last night and this morning he'd left early for work.

"Why weren't they there when we delivered the cupcakes?"

"Thelma said she got an anonymous tip off about a big news story. Something about a secret vote about to happen with the town council that morning. She told her boss, Phil, who rushed out to cover it but Thelma insisted on accompanying him, saying she was the one with the tip. He didn't want to waste time arguing, so she tagged along. She said she'd forgotten about you bringing the cupcakes over in the excitement of getting "a red hot lead"."

"And was there a story about the town council?

"No." He shook his head. "It was a ruse to get them out of the office so the killer could murder Cee Cee."

"Poor Cee Cee."

"Yeah. I also need to go through her gossip columns, and see if there's a hint somewhere as to why someone would kill her. I also need to interview Phil's wife. She sounds like she knew Cee Cee best out of everyone in Gold Leaf Valley."

"Cee Cee told us that she went to college with Phil's wife," Lauren replied. "And that they used to read celebrity gossip together."

"Thanks." He smiled at her. "Let me know if you hear anything else like that."

"Of course."

"Brrt!"

CHAPTER 8

They met up with Zoe and Chris at the local Episcopalian church the next morning. Chris did look a little tired, although that didn't diminish his even, attractive features or his ready smile for them.

The four of them wore outfits suitable to church – slacks and jackets for the guys, while Lauren wore her teal wrap dress, and Zoe wore a lavender skirt and white blouse – a little different from her usual style.

"Zoe is going to show me Zoe Two tomorrow," Chris told them.

"If the paint job is finished," Zoe said. "I'll call Gus tomorrow to check."

"How's the overtime going?" Mitch asked. He and Chris had been friends for years, before Chris had met Zoe.

Chris grimaced. "I'm glad it's available, but I'll also be glad when I have enough saved for our honeymoon." His expression changed when he looked at Zoe. "I can't wait to whisk you away somewhere."

"Me neither." She smiled at him and caught his hand in hers. "Thank you."

Chris tenderly kissed her hand. Zoe blushed faintly.

Father Mike greeted them. Balding and middle-aged, he was beloved by the whole town. "Mrs. Snuggle is looking forward to her playdate with Annie and AJ." He smiled.

"I'm looking forward to it, too." Zoe grinned. "It's going to be so much fun. Hopefully they can act out a scene from my script so I can check if it will work."

Father Mike chuckled. "I'll let Mrs. Snuggle know."

The white Persian had been a former show cat and queen who had needed a new home when her owner had been murdered. Her full name was Mrs. Snuggle Face Furry Frost but everyone called her Mrs. Snuggle for short. Father Mike offered to adopt the grumpy feline, and his kindness to her had made her see that humans could be good. In return, she'd gradually softened and was now devoted to him, although she still had her anti-social moments.

After church, which included a sermon on having faith when you least expect it, Lauren and Zoe proposed to visit Mrs. Finch with Annie, while the guys hung out together.

"And then we could all have lunch at Gary's Burger Diner," Zoe suggested.

"Great idea." Chris smiled at her.

"Yeah. We haven't visited Gary's for a while," Mitch said.

"Because we've all been busy," Lauren said ruefully.

When they returned to the cottage, Lauren buckled Annie into her lavender harness.

"We're visiting Mrs. Finch," Zoe told her.

"Brrt!" *Good.*

They walked the short distance to their friend's house. It was a beautiful day, with a cool breeze ruffling Lauren's shoulder length hair.

After making Mrs. Finch a latte and chatting with her for about thirty minutes, they said goodbye. She promised to visit them on Tuesday at the café.

"What are we doing tomorrow?" Zoe asked as they left their friend's house.

"Brooke is trimming my hair, and I thought you were showing Zoe Two to Chris," Lauren replied.

They usually spent their Monday off together, doing grocery shopping and whatever else cropped up. So far that hadn't changed, even after their weddings.

"Oh, yeah." Zoe pulled her phone out of her purse and made a note. "I'll call Gus first thing tomorrow morning to see if the paint job is done, since he hasn't called me yet."

After taking Annie home, they joined the guys at Gary's Burger Diner, the best place in town for a hamburger. They all ordered the smoky barbecue special with fries, onion rings, and thick shakes. Lauren didn't think she'd need any dinner that night or the next day, either.

***

The next morning, Lauren visited Brooke's hair salon. It felt a little strange doing something on her own without her cousin by her side.

"Hi, Lauren." Brooke wore black jeans and an elegant emerald T-shirt. Her chestnut locks had attractive reddish highlights, cut in a long bob with feathered ends, the color flattering her friendly green eyes. She ushered her to a chair right away. The small salon was empty apart from the two of them.

"Where's Zoe?"

Lauren explained about her possibly buying a car that morning after it was painted a Zoe red.

Brooke laughed. "I can just see Zoe zooming along in a car like that."

"So can I."

After agreeing to a small trim, she relaxed in the chair while Brooke started snipping.

"I love your natural gold highlights," the stylist complimented. "I wish I had those. They look good with your hazel eyes."

"But I think your hair is great," Lauren replied.

"Thanks." Brooke smiled at her in the mirror. "I guess you've heard the news about Cee Cee."

"That she was killed?"

Brooke nodded.

"Unfortunately, Zoe and I found her."

"Oh, no!"

Lauren filled her in, ending with, "I usually read her column but I might have missed a snippet here or there."

"I know what you mean," Brooke agreed, checking the length of her strands, "although I had fun working out who she was talking about. And when she mentioned you had a new cupcake."

"I'm making something this week," Lauren promised.

"Tell me," Brooke urged with a smile.

"You'll have to visit the café," she teased.

After paying Brooke, who said she would definitely visit that week to check out the new creation, Lauren went to the grocery store, then returned to the cottage.

"Brrt?" Annie inquired, sticking her head into the paper grocery sacks on the kitchen table.

"Yes, I've bought your food." Lauren pulled out small cans of her fur baby's favorite brand and placed them in front of her.

"Brrp." *Thank you.* She inspected each label, as if to make sure they were the right ones.

"We're going to make a new cupcake this afternoon."

"Brrt!" Annie sat up straight on the kitchen chair, giving her an approving look.

After Lauren put away the groceries, she and Annie enjoyed their lunch – green salad with tuna for Lauren, and turkey in gravy for Annie.

She cleared the table after lunch and got out her mixer. Although she made the cupcakes in the cafe's commercial kitchen, it was fun making a test batch at home, with Annie helping – and sharing the results with Zoe, Mitch, and Chris.

An electric buzz filled the kitchen as she beat butter and sugar together, then added the eggs and good quality vanilla extract. After folding through the flour and baking powder, the mixture was ready to bake.

She'd just slid the cupcakes in the oven, when there was a knock on the back door.

"Brrt!" Annie ran to the stout wooden door.

"It's me!" Zoe called.

"Come in. Cupcakes will be ready in about twenty minutes."

"Awesome!" Zoe entered, beaming, then her expression fell.

"What's wrong? Did you take Chris to see Zoe Two?"

"Yes." Zoe sank onto a kitchen chair. "I was so excited, and it was the perfect Zoe red, but … I don't know."

"What do you mean?"

"Brrt?" Annie peered at her, and gently patted her arm.

"Thanks." Zoe stroked the Norwegian Forest Cat. "You know how I wasn't very impressed at first with the car last week, and then I got excited about it being painted red?"

"Yes."

"Well, when I showed Chris – who was more enthusiastic about it this morning than I was, by the way – those indecisive feelings came up again. And I'm not used to being—"

"Indecisive." Lauren nodded. It was true.

"We even took it for another test drive and it was fun, but … I wasn't sure. And I know Chris has been tired lately with all the overtime he's been working. I talked to him last night about it but he's determined to save enough for our honeymoon. So," she drew in a breath, "I decided thirty minutes ago I'm not going to buy Zoe Two. Instead, I'm going to put the money into our honeymoon fund and surprise Chris."

"Are you sure?" Lauren asked.

"Brrt?"

"Yes." Zoe nodded. "This decision makes me happier than if I were to buy Zoe Two. Maybe another car will come along, or if I sell my screenplay one day, I can buy myself the perfect Zoe Two. In the meanwhile, I'll make a new batch of pottery mugs to make a bit of extra money and start saving again."

"Have you told Chris?"

"Not yet." Zoe sighed. "I don't want to hurt his feelings because he's set on providing a honeymoon for us, but I don't want him overworking himself, either."

"Then tell him exactly that," Lauren urged. "I'm sure he'll understand. He loves you."

"And I love him." Zoe's face brightened. "Thanks. I'll talk to him tonight."

"How did Gus take the news about not wanting the car?"

"He was okay about it," Zoe replied. "Really good, actually. When I told him I wasn't sure and I'd have to think about it, he said he understood. And when we were leaving, a guy came to get his car fixed and couldn't take his eyes off Zoe Two. In fact, I'll call Gus right now to let him know I don't want her."

Zoe did so, Lauren and Annie hearing her side of the conversation.

"He said no problem." Zoe put her phone away with a smile. "He told me that guy I just mentioned to you made an offer for her, and he was waiting for me to let him know if I was going to buy her. So I feel a lot better now – I hope that other guy gets her."

"Brrt!"

When the oven timer dinged, Lauren took the cupcakes out of the oven. The whole kitchen smelled like good home baking.

"They look amazing." Zoe admired the well-risen golden tops of the cakes.

"Thanks." Lauren smiled. "We need to wait for them to cool."

"Are you sure?" Zoe eyed the tray. "I bet I could handle a hot one."

"If you want to chance it." Lauren remembered that Zoe had burned her fingers once on a fresh from the oven cupcake. "But don't burn your—"

Too late.

"Ouch! Hot!" Zoe snatched a cupcake and juggled it between her hands. She dumped it on the table and then cautiously broke off a piece and popped it in her mouth. "Bud dedicious," she said in a muffled tone. After she chewed and swallowed, she asked, "What are you going to do with them?"

She explained her idea. "I'm going to add lilac frosting and decorate them with white fondant daisies with yellow centers."

"Brrt," Annie said in approval.

The trio chatted about their day as the cupcakes cooled. Then Lauren decorated them, including the little daisy flowers she cut out from the fondant.

"They are so pretty!" Zoe admired the treats. "Now they look too gorgeous to eat!"

"I hope not," Lauren teased. "Otherwise, our profits will go down this week!"

CHAPTER 9

The next morning, Zoe, humming a cheerful tune, unstacked the pine chairs,

"You're in a good mood," Lauren observed. "Not that you usually aren't."

"I spoke to Chris last night." Zoe beamed. "And he was okay with me contributing my car money to our honeymoon fund. More than okay."

"I'm glad."

"Brrt!"

"We might even have enough money now to book our honeymoon. Tonight we're going to look online for any special deals and decide where to go."

"That's great." Lauren smiled.

"It is, isn't it?" Zoe giggled. "I'm so glad I talked to him about it – you were right. Ooh—" another thought seemed to occur to her "–I've ordered something special and it's supposed to be delivered to the café today. I can't wait!"

"What is it?"

"You'll see." Zoe tried to look mysterious but her excited expression ruined the effect.

They finished getting the café ready. Lauren had started baking a little earlier than usual, as she had the special flowers to make for her new creation, which she'd decided to call daisy cupcakes.

When they opened on the dot of nine-thirty, Lauren was dismayed to see Detective Castern walk in.

"What's he doing here?" Zoe muttered to her.

"Brrp?" Annie wrinkled her furry brow and didn't move from her basket. Her previous attempts to befriend Mitch's colleague had been rebuffed.

"Detective Castern." Lauren nodded. Mitch had to work with him. She wanted to be polite.

"I've had reports of a pickpocket acting suspiciously around here. It sounds like he's operating right outside your café." The middle-aged man didn't waste any time on niceties.

"When?" Lauren asked.

"Yes, when?" Zoe wanted to know.

He dug into his jacket pocket – and dug – and dug. He scowled, and practically turned his breast pocket inside out.

"Missing something?" Zoe asked sweetly.

"Zoe." Lauren nudged her warningly.

"My notebook was in this pocket." He looked bewildered. "Where is it?"

"I have no idea," Lauren replied.

"I know I put it in here this morning," he gritted.

"Maybe you met the pickpocket outside," Zoe suggested. "And he – or she – got you!"

"What do you know about it?" he growled, giving up the attempt to find his notebook. He stepped closer to the counter.

Annie's ears pricked and she looked at him in concern. Her fur started rising. Lauren sent her an *it's okay* glance, hoping it *was* okay.

"I don't know anything, apart from what Mitch told Lauren, and she told me," Zoe replied.

"And I don't know anything, either," Lauren said. "Except that you think the pickpocket doesn't operate on the weekends."

"That's right." He nodded. "And you don't open on Mondays."

"That's right," Lauren tried to make her tone pleasant.

"So, by a process of elimination, that means that *you* mean the pickpocket was in the area last week." Zoe glanced around the room. "We certainly didn't notice anyone acting suspiciously in here."

"Neither did Annie. And we haven't received any reports of a customer missing a wallet or their phone."

He grunted. "Maybe they don't know they've been pickpocketed yet."

"Did someone make a report at the police station?" Lauren asked.

"Yes, how else would you know that the pickpocket was close by? We didn't."

"And you call yourself amateur sleuths." It sounded like a sneer.

"I don't," Lauren said, although she supposed that's what they were. A reluctant one, in her case.

"Amateurs that are more successful than the professionals," Zoe put in.

Lauren looked at her in warning.

"Sometimes," Zoe finally amended.

"How I know is confidential," he replied. "You two better be careful – you don't want word getting around town that a criminal likes hanging out near your café."

"A criminal that seems to have picked your pocket this morning," Zoe reminded him.

It looked like steam was about to come out of his ears. His jaw worked, as if he were about to say something nasty, then seemed to think better of it. He stomped out of the café without another word.

"Phew!" Zoe sank down on a stool.

"Brrt?" Annie trotted over to the counter and looked inquiringly at Lauren.

"It's okay." She stepped around the counter and picked up her fur baby. "Good girl. I didn't want you to do anything to him – just watch him."

"Yeah, the bad man's gone now." Zoe nodded vigorously.

"I have no idea how he's a detective," Lauren said, feeling better now with Annie in her arms, the velvety fur soft against her fingertips, "but remember that Mitch has to work with him."

"Sorry. Sometimes I forget." Zoe grimaced. "I have no idea how he puts up with that incompetent guy."

"I know. But I don't want to make Mitch's job any harder than it already is. He enjoys the challenge of it, except for having to deal with *him.*"

"Okay." Zoe nodded. "I promise to try and be good if we run into him again – or if he runs into us."

"Brrt!"

After a moment, Zoe added, "But it looks like Castern made up that stuff about the pickpocket hanging around near us. Don't you think?"

"I do. Surely Mitch would have told me if someone had made a report at the station. Or, if they'd thought they'd lost something in here, they would have asked us if Annie had found it."

"Brrt!"

***

Mrs. Finch came in that morning. After Detective Castern's visit, it was lovely to see her.

"Would you like to try one of my new daisy cupcakes?" Lauren asked.

Annie had already shown their friend to a four-seater near the counter and sat opposite her.

"I would love to, Lauren, dear." Mrs. Finch beamed at them. Today she wore a blue skirt and cream blouse, her gray hair caught up in a slightly untidy bun.

"What would you like to drink?" Zoe's eyes sparkled. "You must try our new pumpkin spice marshmallow mocha!"

"I can't believe we forgot to tell you about it at craft club," Lauren admitted.

"That's because we had lots of other news," Zoe reminded her.

"It sounds too tempting to resist." Mrs. Finch smiled at the trio.

Lauren made the specialty drink, while Zoe plated the daisy cupcake.

They brought their friend's order over to her.

"Something smells delicious." Mrs. Finch gazed down at her mug; the micro foam decorated with chocolate powder.

"If you don't like it, I'll make you something else," Lauren promised.

"I'm sure I'll enjoy it," Mrs. Finch told her. "And my, look at your new cupcake. It really is a work of art with those little white flowers with the yellow centers. It must have taken you a while to make them."

"It did," she admitted. Unfortunately, what had seemed fun yesterday afternoon experimenting with a new creation had translated into a little more work than she'd expected, with cutting out all the fondant flowers.

Lauren watched as Mrs. Finch took her first sip, holding the mug with wobbly hands.

"What an unusual flavor," she praised. "But it's very pleasing."

"Thank you." Lauren smiled.

"Brrt!"

"The pumpkin spice and marshmallows were Zoe's ideas."

"And adding the hot chocolate powder was Lauren's."

"You two – three—" she glanced at Annie "—are very creative."

"Thanks." Zoe looked pleased. "I'm going to make a new mug design soon."

"Oh, what happened with the car you wanted to buy from the mechanic?" Mrs. Finch inquired. "Did you like the Zoe red color?"

Zoe launched into the story of deciding not to buy the car after all, finishing on an upbeat note about her upcoming honeymoon. "We can't wait!" She grinned.

"I'm sure you two will have a lovely time. Lauren, what will you do while Zoe is on vacation?"

"I haven't really thought about it," she admitted, glancing at Annie. "I'm sure Annie and I can manage, and I know Ed will lend a hand serving customers if I need him to."

"Brrt." *Good idea.*

More customers entered. Lauren and Zoe made their apologies and returned to the counter, while Annie seated the newcomers, rejoining Mrs. Finch when she'd completed her hostess duties.

When Mrs. Finch finished her treats, Annie accompanied her to the register. "That was certainly delicious," their friend praised. "I think your pumpkin spice coffee might be my new favorite."

"Even better than a pot of tea?" Zoe teased gently.

"Perhaps." Mrs. Finch nodded.

"Are you okay to walk home?" Lauren eyed their friend's walking stick. "It's no problem to drive you – it will only take a minute."

"I'll be fine, dear," Mrs. Finch reassured her. "Don't worry about me. Besides, my doctor said walking is good for me – it will help keep me limber."

Annie escorted her to the oak and glass entrance door.

They waved goodbye to her, and returned to their customers, until a delivery man appeared in the doorway.

"Package for Zoe Crenshaw."

"That's me!" Zoe rounded the counter and zipped toward him. While Lauren had taken Mitch's last name, her cousin had kept her maiden name. She signed for the large box, and carried it to a spare table.

"What is it?" Lauren eyed the box curiously. Luckily, they didn't have any current orders to attend to.

"Brrt?" *Yes, what is it?* Annie hopped onto the chair next to the box and sniffed at the cardboard.

"You'll see!" Zoe's brown eyes sparkled. She tore open the

packaging. "Ta-da!" Gesturing to the inner box like a hand model, her expression was expectant.

"It says it's an air fryer." Lauren stared at the box.

"Brrt?" *What's that?*

"It's supposed to be *amazing*," Zoe enthused. "It's like a mini oven or something."

"But you don't cook – much. Apart from your pizzas," Lauren added hastily. Which her cousin created with a readymade base.

"This air fryer is going to change that. You can cook tons of things in it, just like you would in an oven, but you can also cook other things you probably wouldn't cook in an oven."

"Like what?"

"Like – like steak!" Zoe finished triumphantly. "Yeah, there are a lot of air fryer steak recipes online, plus pizza recipes, and pork, and chicken. I'm going to make my own fries as well!"

"You can make French fries in that?" The appliance looked tall, oval, and plastic.

"That's what they say." Zoe patted the box. "I can't wait to get this baby home and try it out. But I'll have to wait until tonight. Ooh – I can cook Chris steak for dinner!"

Lauren didn't like to say that the last steak Zoe cooked had ended up in disaster.

"This has a timer on it." Zoe pointed to the description on the packaging as if reading Lauren's mind. "So I won't be able to burn anything!"

"I hope it does what it's supposed to." She'd heard of air fryers, but since she had an oven, microwave, and a stove and grill in the cottage, she hadn't really thought about getting one.

"It will," Zoe replied with supreme confidence. "I watched videos online while Chris was working, and it looks super easy to use. And I bought a big one, so I can fit plenty of food in it! You should get one, too," Zoe urged.

"I think I'll wait and see first," Lauren replied.

"Once I've got the hang of it, you can come over and I'll give you a lesson." Zoe giggled.

"I'd like that." Lauren smiled.

"Brrt!" *Me too!*

***

Ms. Tobin visited in the early afternoon, looking somber. She wore an amber skirt and cream blouse, the color combination suiting her brown hair.

"Brrt?" Annie trotted over to greet her.

"Hello, Annie, dear." She managed a smile for the feline. "Where should I sit?"

"Hi, Ms. Tobin," Zoe greeted her with a big smile.

"Hi," Lauren replied pleasantly.

"Hello, girls. It's a bad business about Cee Cee, isn't it?"

"How did you find out?" Zoe asked.

"My friend at the senior center told me. And it was in this morning's issue of the *Gold Leaf Valley Gazette*."

"Oh, that's right." Lauren had forgotten that the newspaper came out on Tuesdays.

"Do you have a copy?" Zoe asked.

"Yes." Ms. Tobin reached into her tote bag. "Here you go."

"What does it say?" Zoe came around the counter, Lauren following.

Death of our gossip columnist, stated the headline on the front page.

"Didn't I tell you girls? One wrong word and someone's feelings could get hurt."

"It looks like you were right," Lauren agreed.

"Has Mitch got any leads yet?" Zoe turned to her.

"No." He hadn't spoken to her about the case since Saturday night. "Not that I'm aware of."

"I wonder if the gossip column is in this week's issue." Zoe flicked the pages. "Nope, can't see it. Oh, wait. There's a little paragraph saying they hope the gossip section will resume shortly."

Lauren peered over her cousin's shoulder. Yes, that was exactly what it said.

"I don't think that's a good idea." Ms. Tobin shook her head. "You'd think they would learn from this." After a moment, she asked, "Did you hear there's a pickpocket in town?"

"Yes, but how did you know?" Zoe asked.

"The senior center again. One of the members reported his wallet stolen – it must have happened in the street last week."

"No one has reported being targeted while they've been here, have they?" Lauren was mindful of Detective Castern's accusation earlier that day.

"Not that I'm aware," Ms. Tobin replied. "Why?"

"It looks like Detective Castern was a victim this morning." Zoe launched into the tale.

"I'm afraid I do not like that fellow," Ms. Tobin commented. "It doesn't say much about his detective abilities if he's a victim of this pickpocket as well."

"Exactly!" Zoe sounded pleased.

"What would you like to order?" Lauren asked.

"I would love to try your new pumpkin spice coffee," Ms. Tobin replied. "Martha has been enthusing about it at the senior center."

"I also have a new daisy cupcake." Lauren gestured to the glass counter.

"They're so cute! You must try one," Zoe urged.

"Very well." Ms. Tobin smiled. "Zoe, are you going to design any more mugs featuring Annie?"

"Yes," Zoe replied. "I'm just trying to come up with the perfect idea."

"Please tell me when they're ready," Ms. Tobin replied. "I must buy one from you."

"I'll definitely let you know." Zoe grinned.

Ms. Tobin had bought each new mug design from Zoe, declaring each creation captured Annie's likeness perfectly.

They returned to the counter to start their friend's order. While Lauren steamed the milk, she could see Annie chattering away to Ms. Tobin.

"She's probably asking what her cat Miranda is up to today," Zoe said.

"Probably," Lauren replied with a smile.

After making the pumpkin spice marshmallow mocha, she brought it over to Ms. Tobin, Zoe accompanying her with the cupcake.

"That looks darling." Ms. Tobin studied the lilac frosting on the cupcake, decorated with fondant flowers. "And this mocha does smell a little different."

"Wait until you taste it," Zoe promised.

Ms. Tobin took a small sip, then smiled. "Martha was right about this drink. I'm glad I took a chance on it."

"It's not too sweet, is it?" Lauren asked.

"No, somehow it just seems to work together perfectly."

"Awesome!" Zoe beamed.

They were able to spend a few minutes chatting to Ms. Tobin before new customers claimed their attention.

Just after three-thirty, Zoe's phone buzzed.

"It's Father Mike. I hope everything's okay." After a brief conversation, she turned to Lauren. "Something's cropped up so he wanted to know if Mrs. Snuggle could come over for her playdate tomorrow afternoon around this time."

Lauren's eyes widened.

"I know, we'll be open then. It was supposed to be tomorrow after work but he needs to visit a parishioner then, and that's the best time for them."

"Of course." Lauren nodded. Father Mike did so much good for everyone – the least she could do was accommodate the new playdate time. And he'd said at church on Sunday that Mrs. Snuggle had been looking forward to seeing Annie again.

"You're the best." Zoe beamed.

"We'll make it work. But check with Ed if that's a good time to bring AJ over as well. He usually finishes in the kitchen around now, anyway."

"Will do." Zoe zipped through the swinging kitchen doors, and zipped back a couple of minutes later. "He said no problem. He also said he can help serve in here if you need him to."

"I should be okay on my own – it's usually not as busy after the lunch rush. I'll go and tell him." Lauren entered the kitchen and had her own conversation with Ed.

"AJ's looking forward to getting together with Annie. Mrs. Snuggle, she's not so sure about." Ed chuckled. "But I'm certain they'll have a lot of fun tomorrow afternoon." He was cleaning up the kitchen. "Are you sure you don't want me to stay and help out?" He nodded toward the café space a wall away.

"Thanks, but I'm sure I'll be fine." Lauren knew he preferred to remain in the kitchen. "It shouldn't get too busy."

"I'll bring AJ over tomorrow at three-thirty, then. I'll have to leave a bit earlier than usual to do that."

"No problem." Lauren smiled. "Thanks for allowing AJ to help Zoe out with her screenplay like this."

"No problem." His teeth flashed briefly. "I don't go in for those sorts of movies but I've seen AJ watching them." He chuckled. "I don't think I'm supposed to know that. But if Zoe's script gets made, of course I would watch it."

Lauren returned to the counter, and they chatted with Annie about tomorrow's playdate.

"It's going to be awesome," Zoe assured the feline. "I'll bring my script and read it to you, and there's one scene in particular I'd like the three of you to act out."

"Brrt!" Annie's green eyes shone with interest.

"Tomorrow is going to be such a fun day." She turned to Lauren. "You'll have to take a break, even if it's for just a minute, to join us."

137

"I will," she promised, now intrigued. She was sure any customers would understand if she departed next door for a very short time.

"Brrt!" *Yes, you will!*

CHAPTER 10

The next morning, Zoe enthused about her new air fryer.

"It's amazing! I cooked the most perfect steak for Chris last night."

"You did?" Lauren looked at her.

"I cooked one for myself too – they both fit in the fryer at once – and it was delicious!"

"Did you hear the timer?" Lauren couldn't resist teasing gently.

"Yep. I was working on my script in the kitchen, and it was loud enough to break my concentration."

"That's good."

"And Chris and I looked at our honeymoon options. We can afford a seven-night cruise to the Caribbean, or a week in Puerto Rico or Florida. Now I'm having trouble deciding."

"What about Chris?" Lauren asked.

"He said he doesn't mind out of those three options. And they all sound good to me. I'm leaning toward a cruise, but I don't want to get seasick. I don't want Chris getting seasick, either."

"That would be a shame," Lauren sympathized.

"Well anyway, we'll have fun deciding." Zoe smiled, then changed the subject. "Hey, did you tell Mitch about Detective Castern getting pickpocketed yesterday morning?"

"I did." Lauren's lips curved with amusement as she remembered her husband's laughter.

"Did he tell you anything new about Cee Cee's murder?"

"Not really." Mitch had been a little frustrated by his lack of progress on the case. "They're checking everyone out who placed an ad in last week's issue."

"That's us!" Zoe stared at her with wide eyes.

"You're right." With everything that had happened, she couldn't believe she'd forgotten. She hadn't even thought of it when they'd looked at Ms. Tobin's copy of the *Gazette* yesterday.

"Is our ad in it?" Zoe zipped to the counter and picked up their issue that she'd bought that morning. Rustling the pages noisily, she stabbed her finger on a back page. "Yep, we are. Right next to Gus, and the handmade shop."

Lauren leaned over her cousin's shoulder and checked the ad. It was exactly as she remembered writing it out at the newspaper office.

"It doesn't seem to have done much for business yesterday," Zoe remarked.

"Give it time," Lauren replied. "People probably have a lot more on their mind since we placed the ad."

"Like Cee Cee's death and the pickpocket." Zoe nodded.

"Brrt!"

There was a knock on the oak and glass door.

Lauren glanced at her watch. "Oops. We should have opened five minutes ago." She hurried over to the door and unbolted it. "Sorry." She found herself apologizing to Gus, the mechanic, wearing old jeans and a faded T-shirt.

"Hi," Zoe greeted him with a smile. "Did that other guy buy Zoe Two?"

"He did." Gus chuckled. "Thanks to your ideas about painting it red. Didn't quibble about the price, either."

"That's great," Lauren said.

"What can we get you?" Lauren glanced around the café for Annie, but her fur baby was nowhere to be seen. Then she vaguely remembered that a few minutes ago, she'd shimmied through the cat flap into the private hallway that led to the cottage. Perhaps she'd wanted some privacy for a moment?

"A large latte sounds good." His gaze strayed to the small chalkboard promoting their pumpkin spice mocha. "That pumpkin drink sounds too fancy for me."

"Everyone loves it so far," Zoe told him.

"Really?" He sounded skeptical. "I'll have to tell my wife. She loves trying new things."

"How about a cupcake?" Zoe gestured to the display case. "Or a Danish? Lauren is famous for her cupcakes, and she's just created a new daisy one, and Ed is famous for his pastries. Today he's made honeyed walnut, one of his most popular creations."

"You're good." He pointed a finger at her. "If you ever want to sell cars, come and see me."

Zoe grinned.

"Would you like your latte to have here or to go?" Lauren asked.

"To go. I'd love to take a real break, but I've got plenty of repairs to keep me busy." He looked around the empty café. "This looks like a nice place to have some peace and quiet."

"It is," Zoe replied, "except when it's busy. Then we're rushed off our feet!"

Lauren created a swan on top of the micro foam, before putting a lid on top of it. The advanced latte art class they'd taken a while ago had really paid off.

"Here you go." She placed it on the counter.

"Thanks." He pulled his wallet out of his jeans' pocket and thumbed it open.

After paying with cash, he looked regretfully at the tempting treats in the glass display. "Maybe I'll get a cupcake next time."

"We'll be here," Zoe said cheerfully.

A couple of minutes later, the cat flap opened, and Annie shimmied through, carrying her little stuffed hedgehog.

"So that's what you were doing." Lauren smiled at her fur baby.

"Brrp," Annie managed, gently depositing her toy in her pink basket, then hopping in as well.

A couple more customers came in. Annie seated them, and returned to her basket. She seemed to know when someone was receptive to her company or not.

Lauren looked up when the door opened again, hoping it was Mitch. Instead, it was a blond stranger, looking smart in a dark suit. Recognition dawned.

"Hey, that's Bryce, the real estate guy who came into the newspaper office after we found Cee Cee," Zoe muttered to her.

"You're right." She nodded.

"This is perfect." Zoe brightened. "We were going to check him out anyway, weren't we? And since Mitch doesn't have any real leads yet, I think it's time we put our sleuthing hats on, don't you?"

"Brrt?" Annie trotted up to him. She'd left her toy in her basket.

"She'll show you to a table," Lauren informed him. "Unless you'd rather take it to go."

He stared down at Annie as if he'd never been to a cat café before. Perhaps he hadn't.

"People told me about this, but I didn't believe them." He laughed and shook his head, before focusing on the cupcakes and Danishes before him. "What's good?"

"Everything," Zoe told him, a touch haughtily.

"I'll have a regular latte to go," he decided after a moment. "And one of those cupcakes. The one with the chocolate on it."

"That's a triple chocolate ganache," Zoe commented. "You'll love it."

"Hope so."

"How do you like Gold Leaf Valley so far?" Lauren asked, steaming the milk.

"It's cute," he replied. "Some of these Victorian houses are ripe for rehabbing. I'm thinking of buying one myself."

"Did you know Cee Cee well? The gossip columnist?"

Lauren frowned at her cousin. Sometimes Zoe wasn't known for her subtlety.

"Brrt?" *Did you?*

"No. I've just moved here." He stared at them. "How about you? You were the ones who found her, weren't you?"

"Unfortunately," Lauren replied. "She seemed like a nice woman."

"Hey!" Zoe snapped her fingers. "Didn't you say at the newspaper office that you had some gossip for Cee Cee?"

"That's right."

"What was it?"

"Why do you want to know?" He frowned.

"Just curious," Zoe replied airily.

"If you must know, I told Thelma instead. She said she'd put it in the next edition, but there wasn't any gossip column this week."

"What was your piece of gossip?" Lauren couldn't help inquiring.

"Just someone who decided to sell their house. It's the first time it's been for sale for over forty years. I was told the locals hang onto their homes for a long time here, but I thought forty years was impressive."

"Who is it?" Zoe persisted.

"Some older man who wants to move to another state to be closer to his adult kids. He said he's not here a lot, anyway." He shrugged.

"That's it?" Zoe scrunched her nose.

"Well, I didn't think much of that wedding bells bit last week. Who cares if someone's getting married?"

"You would if you were a local," Zoe told him.

"Here's your latte and cupcake." Lauren placed the order on the counter.

"Thanks." He paid with a card, the machine making a little beep as it was approved.

"I don't know if I like him." Zoe stared after him, watching him walk down the street past their large window.

"I know what you mean," Lauren replied, "but it can't be easy to move to a strange town where everyone knows everyone else."

"Apart from you – him." Zoe nodded thoughtfully. "Yeah, maybe he's just trying to fit in with giving some gossip to the newspaper."

A flurry of customers demanded their – and Annie's –attention, and then it was the lunch rush. By the time it was over, Lauren definitely needed a short break. Zoe said she'd have her lunch late, during the feline playdate.

She grabbed her meal quickly in the cottage, making it healthy by adding a ton of lettuce leaves to a small can of tuna. Annie joined her, enjoying beef and liver.

"Ready for your playdate with Zoe and the others this afternoon?"

"Brrt!"

They rejoined Zoe in the café.

"Father Mike just called. He'll be here at three-thirty with Mrs. Snuggle." Zoe glanced around the quiet café. A couple of customers shared a table and chatted to each other, enjoying their sweet treats.

Lauren checked her watch. Almost three. "I'll see how Ed's doing." She pushed open the swinging kitchen doors.

Ed was cleaning up his pastry bench. "I'm almost ready to pick up AJ and bring her over."

Lauren glanced around the gleaming kitchen. "It looks good. Thanks."

"I started a little earlier today, so I'd finish before the playdate." An old-fashioned landline tone suddenly rang. He looked startled. "Excuse me. It's my phone."

Lauren stepped out of the kitchen, trying not to eavesdrop, but she couldn't help overhear Ed's gruff voice.

"That should be okay, Rebecca. I have to bring AJ to the café first for a playdate and then I can go and pick him up."

There was silence, and Lauren assumed he'd ended the call.

Ed stuck his shaggy head through the door. "They're shorthanded at the animal shelter today. Rebecca just asked me if I could pick up a stray dog someone's found. So I'll bring AJ over now if that's okay, and then drive out to get the dog."

"Of course." He and AJ regularly volunteered at the shelter, AJ making friends with the cats there, and she knew that he and Rebecca were dating.

"Thanks. I'll leave in a couple of minutes."

She filled Zoe in on the conversation.

"Awesome! I might be able to find a scene for Annie and AJ to act out while we wait for Mrs. Snuggle to arrive."

Another customer entered, and Lauren made a cappuccino for them while Zoe chatted to Annie about her plans for their playdate.

When Ed arrived with AJ, Annie greeted her friend in the cafe.

"Brrt!"

"Meow."

Ed opened up the carrier and the large brown tabby jumped out. Then she looked up at Ed with big eyes.

"Meow?"

"I have to help Rebecca at the animal shelter," he told her gently. "But I want you to have fun with Annie and Mrs. Snuggle on your playdate. I'll come back for you later today."

"Meow." AJ moved her head in a little nod, but looked wistfully after him as he departed.

"AJ and Ed have really bonded," Zoe murmured to Lauren.

"They certainly have."

"Why don't we go into the cottage?" Zoe suggested to the duo. "Mrs. Snuggle should be here soon and then we can act out the scene from my screenplay that I have in mind. And we can also try out another scene while we wait for her."

"Brrt!" Annie trotted toward the private hallway and looked over her shoulder for AJ to join her.

"Meow." The brown tabby sauntered after Annie.

"Will you be okay here?" Zoe waved a hand toward the three diners.

"I'll be fine. I'll let you know when Mrs. Snuggle and Father Mike arrive."

"Awesome!" Zoe followed the cats into the private hallway that led to the cottage, but she entered through the door, not the cat flap.

A few minutes later, one of the diners paid, thanking her for the daisy cupcake and latte. "I'll certainly be back."

"Thanks." She hadn't seen the middle-aged lady before, but it was nice to get some new customers, not that she wasn't grateful for her – their – regulars, most of whom she considered friends.

Was there something on at the senior center? Quiet afternoons weren't uncommon, but today was unusually slow. Hopefully it would give her a chance to join the playdate for a few minutes.

The entrance door opened, and Father Mike walked in, carrying a large carrier.

"Hi, Father Mike," she greeted him. "Hi, Mrs. Snuggle."

The white Persian peered through the gray plastic bars and muttered something that could be taken as a meow.

"Hi, Lauren." Father Mike wore slacks and a blue button-down shirt, looking cool and comfortable.

"Zoe is in the cottage with Annie and AJ." She smiled at the fluffy cat. "Are you ready to join them?"

A grumbly meow.

"I think Mrs. Snuggle is looking forward to it," he assured her. "But sometimes she doesn't express her feelings very well."

"I understand," Lauren replied gently.

She escorted them down the private hallway and into the cottage.

"Mrs. Snuggle is here," she called out cheerfully.

"Brrt!" Annie ran to greet her friend.

"Meow." Mrs. Snuggle sounded friendlier when she spied Annie.

AJ looked at the white Persian curiously.

"Remember Mrs. Snuggle?" Zoe asked the brown tabby. "You've played with her before."

"But mostly cyber playdates," Lauren added.

Father Mike opened the carrier and Mrs. Snuggle neatly climbed out. "Meow?" She glanced up at Father Mike, her blue eyes wide.

"I have to visit a church-goer," he told her softly, "but Annie, Lauren, and Zoe will look after you. I'm sure you'll enjoy playing with AJ, too. I'll pick you up before dinner time tonight."

"Meow." Mrs. Snuggle tilted her head in a way that could be interpreted as a nod.

"We're going to have lots of fun," Zoe told the three felines. "Just you see!"

"Thanks for bringing her over," Lauren said to the priest.

"Thank you for inviting her. I know she regards Annie as a friend."

"And Annie feels the same." She smiled, remembering the way Annie had tried to make the Persian feel at home here when they'd cat sat her for Father Mike a while ago.

Father Mike departed.

"Okay, everyone." Zoe ushered them into the living room. "Now that you're all here, we're going to act out a scene from my script that I've been having trouble with. Annie, you can be the princess, so I need you to sit on the sofa, please."

"Brrt!" Annie looked pleased and hopped up on the pink couch.

"Mrs. Snuggle, I thought you could be Annie's head bodyguard, and protect her."

"Meow." The Persian sounded considering, but didn't seem to reject the idea.

"If you could just stand in front of the sofa, so it's like you're guarding her."

Mrs. Snuggle walked over to Annie, looked up at her in what passed as a friendly manner, and then turned around so she was facing Lauren and Zoe.

"Excellent." Zoe beamed at the Persian. "Now, AJ." She glanced around the room. "Where's AJ?"

"She was here a moment ago." Lauren peered into the hallway. "Oh, she's near the front door." She hurried over to the Maine Coon. "AJ, it's play time now with Zoe's script."

"Meow."

"We really need you to help act out this scene," Zoe told her encouragingly when Lauren brought her back into the living room. "I thought you could be the girl who finds the royal crown. Annie needs that crown to prove that she is the rightful princess, and the next ruler in the line of succession!"

"I can't wait to read your script," Lauren said.

"Thanks." Zoe grinned, then rummaged in a tote bag. "I've even made a crown!" She flourished a piece of gold cardboard. "I cut it out last night. So, AJ, I'll give this to you, and then you can go over to Annie and give it to her, because you want Annie to prove she is the true princess." Zoe looked down at the brown tabby earnestly. "Can you do that?"

"Meow," AJ decided. She sounded encouraging.

"Great." Zoe handed her the shiny gold crown.

AJ took it in her mouth.

"So, you go over to Annie, and hand her the crown. I really need to see if this will work in my script."

AJ ambled over to Annie, sitting on the sofa. Mrs. Snuggle had a forbidding expression on her face, just like a real bodyguard.

"Great acting, Mrs. Snuggle," Zoe praised.

Lauren hoped it *was* acting.

"Brrp?" *Is that for me?* Annie looked encouragingly at AJ.

AJ cast her gaze down at the crown in her mouth, and then up at Annie. A mischievous expression flickered across her furry face.

AJ gave a muffled meow and galloped out of the room, the crown still in her mouth.

"AJ!" Zoe's mouth fell open. She turned to Lauren. "That's not supposed to happen!"

AJ darted down the hall.

"Brrt?" Annie looked at Lauren.

"Meow." Mrs. Snuggle frowned, her white furry face all wrinkled with disapproval.

"AJ!" Lauren hurried down the hall. No brown tabby. "I'll check the bedrooms." She dashed into her bedroom and peered under the bed. "AJ, don't you want to play with the others?"

No answer.

Lauren checked Annie's bedroom, which used to be Zoe's, before her marriage to Chris. No AJ.

"Brrt!" Annie poked her head into the doorway.

"Where is she?" Lauren whispered.

Annie turned and trotted down the hall to the kitchen.

"Meow?" AJ sat in front of Annie's lilac bowl, looking hopeful. Somehow the crown had ended up on her head, tilted at a rakish angle.

"Oh, AJ." Zoe appeared in the doorway. "Why didn't you say you were hungry?" She spied the crown. "Did you want to be the princess? I didn't realize." She glanced at Lauren. "I guess we'd better give them all a snack."

"Good idea."

Mrs. Snuggle's blue eyes lit up at the mention of food, and she joined them in the kitchen.

Lauren grabbed two bowls from the cupboard for the guests, and soon they were all happily licking away at chicken in gravy.

Lauren's phone buzzed. She grabbed it from the kitchen table and shared a surprised look with Zoe. "It's Thelma," she mouthed.

"Lauren, Phil feels terrible that we haven't paid you for the cupcakes last week," the newspaper receptionist said. "Are you able to come into the newspaper office this afternoon? We close at five."

"I'll be there," she promised, and ended the call. Shock suddenly hit her. "I've left the café unattended!"

"All the time you've been here?" Zoe's eyes rounded. "I assumed you must have locked up."

"I thought I'd only be in here a minute." She rushed down the private hallway and into the café. Zoe followed.

The last two customers were gone, and money was placed next to the register.

She opened the drawer and looked at the notes and coins inside, and then at the card machine. Everything looked correct.

"Phew." She shook her head. "I can't believe I did that."

"I can. You were having fun with the cats. Just like I was." Zoe paused. "Until AJ decided to act out the scene in her own way."

"She's always been independent," Lauren said ruefully, remembering the time they'd tried training her as Annie's assistant. It was something they still laughed about occasionally.

"True. Well, from the limited acting out they did, I think that scene will work, after all. As long as the girl in the story doesn't run off with the crown – ooh, wait. Maybe she does run off with the crown because she wants to be a princess and the real princess and the bodyguard have to chase her!" Zoe's eyes sparkled with inspiration. "Thanks, AJ!"

Lauren smiled. "Since there aren't any customers, maybe we should close early for once." She didn't usually like doing that, but with the cats in the cottage, and needing to visit the *Gazette* office, there didn't seem to be much choice.

"Good idea. Where are you going, anyway? When you told Thelma you'd be there?" Zoe asked curiously.

"Thelma said they want to pay for last week's cupcakes."

"Awesome! I'll go with you."

"What about the cats?" Lauren looked over at the private hallway. "We can't just leave them alone – can we?"

"Annie's a good hostess and we – you – leave her alone when you need to. I'm sure Mrs. Snuggle and AJ will behave." A sudden thought seemed to strike her and she dug out her phone from her jeans' pocket. "I know! We can record them! We can set up the camera on one phone, and watch them with the other phone. Just like we do on a cyber playdate with Annie and Mrs. Snuggle, or AJ."

"Great idea." Lauren felt better about dashing over to the *Gazette* office. She called Zoe on her device.

"All set. Point your phone over there." Zoe gestured to the espresso machine.

Lauren did so.

"It's working. The espresso machine is appearing on my phone."

"That is—"

"Genius, if I do say so myself." Zoe giggled. "So, we can leave your phone in the cottage keeping an eye on the cats, and we'll be able to watch them with mine!"

"As long as we're not gone too long," Lauren warned. "We're responsible for Mrs. Snuggle and AJ during this playdate."

"I know." Zoe nodded. "We'll just dash to the newspaper office and dash back. I promise."

"Well, all right." She hoped it would be as simple as Zoe made it sound. "But we'd better tell Annie and the others what's happening."

They returned to the cottage, outlining the plan for the trio.

"Annie's in charge," Lauren finished. "Are you okay with that?" she asked her fur baby.

"Brrt!" *Yes!*

"And we'll be watching you with the phone camera." Zoe pointed to Lauren's. "Like when you have a playdate on the phone with Annie, and you can see each other playing."

"Meow." Mrs. Snuggle sounded slightly agreeable.

AJ didn't say anything, busily licking her bowl clean, and then licking the others, which didn't seem to have a scrap of food left in them.

"So, I think you three should play in the living room," Lauren suggested.

"Brrt!" *Good idea.*

Lauren smiled at Annie, watching her shepherd her playmates into the living room.

"We won't be long," Lauren called, making sure she locked the door behind her and Zoe.

"See? They're having fun already." Zoe showed her the phone screen. The three felines were playing with Annie's jingle balls.

"Good." Lauren nodded. "Let's go!"

They jogged around the corner to the newspaper office.

"Hi, Thelma." Lauren was slightly out of breath as she approached the reception desk.

"Hi." Thelma smiled at them. "Thanks for coming. We feel terrible we didn't pay you last week for the cupcakes, but with everything that happened with Cee Cee …"

"I understand." Lauren nodded.

"Let me just get the money from the boss." She rolled her eyes. "He has to approve everything. I've told him that in other offices the receptionist or secretary handles the petty cash, and since he doesn't have a secretary, I should be in charge of it, but he says every little thing has to be accounted for. Honestly." She shook her head. "The reason you have petty cash is so you don't have to account for every little item."

"Hey, did you get my voicemail last week?" Zoe asked her. "About there being a pickpocket in town?"

"I certainly did." Thelma nodded. "Thanks. I've already written the article – and spoken to the police department about it. Now my boss is going over it." She held up crossed fingers. "I hope he publishes it. I told him we were doing a public service by letting everyone know about it."

"I think you are," Lauren replied.

"Yeah, I spoke to a Detective Castern – he's a grumpy guy, isn't he?" Thelma shook her head. "He said he was going to catch this pickpocket but he wouldn't tell me anything else. He promised he'd call me as soon as he'd made an arrest, but I'm still waiting." She tapped the landline phone on her desk.

"What about the gossip column?" Zoe wanted to know. "We checked the *Gazette* but there wasn't one this week, just a short message that it wasn't running in this issue."

"I'm working on it." Thelma frowned. "I'm still trying to convince the boss I'm the right person for the job. Now he's suddenly talking about hiring someone else to do it." Her eyes narrowed. "If he does, that's it! I'm out of here."

"Thelma!" Phil poked his head out of the inner office. "Here's the cupcake money for when they get—"

He looked at Lauren and Zoe in surprise. "You're here."

"Just arrived," Zoe informed him.

"Good, good." He handed a handful of cash to Thelma. "Sorry we didn't pay you last week but with poor Cee Cee's death—"

An elegant woman suddenly emerged from the inner office. She wore a pale pink floral dress that flattered her slim figure.

"You must be Lauren and Zoe." She smiled at them. "Cee Cee told me she enjoyed going to your café. I'm Katherine, Phil's wife."

"Hello." Lauren smiled in return.

"I can't believe my friend is dead." She shook her head. "I thought I was doing her a favor getting her this job, but now look how it's turned out!" Sorrow flickered across her face.

"The police are doing everything they can," her husband told her. "Detective Denman seems to know what he's doing."

"Yes. He does. I just wish he was in charge of catching this pickpocket as well. A friend from the tennis club said their wallet was stolen from the change room last week."

"Really?" Thelma jumped into the conversation. "Detective Castern didn't tell me that. For my article," she added, when Katherine furrowed her brow.

"I do wish you'd publish the article, dear," Katherine told her husband. "I already have a couple of friends asking why there's nothing in the *Gazette* about this criminal."

"You know I like assembling all the facts first," Phil told her a little testily, his gaze swinging toward Lauren and Zoe, before turning back to her. "We can talk about this tonight."

"Of course." Katherine nodded, then turned to Lauren and Zoe. "It was nice meeting you two. I must stop by your café one day." She stepped around the reception desk and waved goodbye to her husband.

Phil retreated into his office, closing the door behind him.

"Here you go." Thelma handed Lauren the handful of cash.

She counted it quickly, as the wad seemed a little big. "It's too much." Lauren peeled off a couple of one-dollar notes and held them out to Thelma.

The phone rang, and Thelma answered it immediately. "*Gold Leaf Valley Gazette*. How may I help you?" She gestured to Lauren to go into the office with the change. "Uh-huh, yes, I understand. Really? We'll definitely investigate that." Thelma continued to listen to the caller, waving her hand toward the office again.

Lauren glanced at Zoe, and shrugged. They stepped behind the reception desk, and then she knocked on the inner door.

"Excuse me, Phil?" she called softly, not wanting to disturb Thelma's phone call.

Zoe knocked a little more forcefully, then opened the door.

Phil looked up, startled. He slammed his desk drawer shut. "What is it?"

"Sorry to disturb you," Lauren said apologetically.

"We did knock," Zoe added.

"Come in." He beckoned them in.

"You paid us too much." Lauren held out two dollars.

"Keep it. Consider it commission."

"Thank you, but—"

"Thanks," Zoe said brightly. She pushed Lauren's outstretched hand down. "Let us know when we can deliver cupcakes again."

"Soon, if Thelma has her way." He forced a chuckle. "They were good."

"I'm glad you liked them." Lauren urged Zoe back into the reception area.

"All set?" Thelma had finished her phone call.

"Yes." Lauren smiled at her. "We'd better get going."

"Let's check what the cats are up to on their playdate." Zoe dug out her phone. She was silent for a moment.

"What?" Lauren peered over her shoulder. The living room was empty.

"Maybe they're drinking some water in the kitchen," Zoe suggested hopefully.

"We'd better get back." Lauren's heart started to pound. She told herself she was being silly. There was no way the cats could leave the cottage – but had she locked the cat flap on the back door? She trusted Annie to look after Mrs. Snuggle and AJ, but had a sudden flashback to when they had cat sat Mrs. Snuggle, the Persian determined to return home – by walking from the cottage to the parsonage, Annie keeping her company.

Meeting her cousin's gaze, they nodded at the same time and dashed back to the café.

"I see them!" Zoe put on a burst of speed and nearly skidded into Ms. Tobin.

The three felines were on the inside of the glass door, staring up at that lady on the outside.

"What's going on, girls?" Ms. Tobin observed their flushed faces and puffed breathing. "Is it cats only this afternoon?" She sounded amused.

"Sort of," Lauren replied. "I'm sorry, we were just at the newspaper office for a minute – well, it was supposed to be a minute."

"And Annie is having a playdate." Zoe gestured to the trio, now scrutinizing them as well.

"Why don't we go inside?" Lauren suggested. "I'll have to unlock from in there. Then we'll make you a latte – on the house."

"You don't have to do that," Ms. Tobin replied. "Why don't you tell me what's going on instead?"

"We will in a jiffy," Zoe promised.

They rushed around the back and entered the café through the commercial kitchen. It was a quicker way to enter the coffee shop than through the cottage and connecting private hallway.

"What have you three been up to?" Lauren glanced down at her fur baby, and then Mrs. Snuggle and AJ. She was just relieved they hadn't wandered any further, and made a mental note to *always* supervise a live playdate.

AJ tried to look demure but failed, and Mrs. Snuggle looked a little less grumpy than usual, as if she'd enjoyed their illicit foray into the café.

"You two knew Annie was in charge while we were gone," Lauren reminded them.

"Maybe they sensed Ms. Tobin was outside and they wanted to let her in," Zoe suggested.

"Brrt!" *That's right!*

"How were you going to reach up here?" Lauren slid the bolt back at the top of the door.

"I bet they were going to stand on each other's backs." Zoe giggled.

Lauren hastily let in Ms. Tobin, who still looked amused, and then encouraged the cats away from the entrance.

"We'd better take them back to the living room," she suggested.

"I'll go." Zoe urged the cats to follow her. "You guys still have some playdate time left."

"Maybe you should supervise," Lauren called after her.

"Good idea!"

She hastily made a large latte for Ms. Tobin and filled her in on the playdate.

"I'm glad Annie is having fun." She smiled as she sipped her latte. "I'd love to have a cupcake as well, but I want to enjoy my dinner tonight. I'm making chocolate mousse for myself for dessert."

"That sounds delicious." Lauren's mouth watered at the thought. Perhaps she should make it too that evening – it would be a treat for Mitch – and herself.

Father Mike entered the café. "I hope I wasn't gone too long." He glanced around the room, empty apart from Ms. Tobin.

"No, AJ is still here as well."

"Did Mrs. Snuggle enjoy herself?" He looked hopeful.

"I think so. She was great at acting the part of Annie's bodyguard in the scene Zoe asked them to help her with."

He chuckled. "I can just imagine that."

After saying hello to Ms. Tobin, he accompanied Lauren through the private hallway to the cottage. He'd just put Mrs. Snuggle into her carrier when there was a knock at the back door.

Ed stood in the doorway.

"Meow!" AJ ran to him, and stretched her top paws gently on his leg.

"Did you miss me?" He chuckled as he picked her up. His face was almost obscured by her bushy brown tail. "I hope she was good for you guys," Ed said.

Lauren and Zoe looked at each other.

"Pretty good," Zoe replied. "She really helped me out with the scene from the script. In fact, she's given me a new idea for it!"

"Really?" Ed looked at his Maine Coon proudly. "Did you hear that?"

"Meow!" AJ sounded pleased.

The two men left, Annie saying goodbye to both of her friends, then Lauren ran back to the café, making her apologies to Ms. Tobin.

"No need to worry. No one else came in."

"Good." Lauren leaned against the edge of the counter. "Is there something going on at the senior center today? Business has been slower than usual." Not that she should complain – the lack of customers had been convenient for the playdate and the dash to the *Gazette* office.

"I think there's a martial arts demonstration," Ms. Tobin replied. "Not my sort of thing, I'm afraid."

She wondered if Martha had attended – she could just imagine their older friend cheering with every move the expert showed.

"I'm back." Zoe rushed into the café, followed by Annie.

The silver-gray tabby trotted over to Ms. Tobin's table and hopped up on the chair opposite her.

"How are the mug designs coming along?" Ms. Tobin asked.

"I've just had the greatest idea." Zoe grinned. "A mug with all three cats on them – Annie, Mrs. Snuggle, and AJ!"

"Brrt!"

"I'll have to ask Father Mike and Ed if that's okay with them, and I'll split some of the profits with them."

"It sounds like a marvelous idea," Ms. Tobin approved. "I can't wait until they're ready. I would love to be the first to buy one."

Zoe pulled out her phone from her jeans' pocket and made a note. "Thanks, Ms. Tobin."

"Thank *you*, Zoe. Your mugs definitely brighten up my kitchen."

Zoe beamed at her. Once again, Lauren marveled at how their prickliest customer a few years ago had now become a kind friend to them.

When Ms. Tobin left, Lauren made them both a latte.

"I definitely need this." Zoe hopped up on a stool behind the counter and dangled her sneaker-clad feet.

"Me too." Lauren glanced at the empty tables and chairs. For once, she hoped no one else came in before closing. Annie had ambled to her pink basket and snoozed, curled up in a silver-gray ball.

She checked her watch. Only twenty minutes to go until they could lock up and start cleaning. She sighed. That was not one of her favorite tasks, but the sooner they got it done, the sooner they could relax.

The door opened, and Thelma walked in.

"Brrt?" Annie lifted her head for a second, then went back to sleep.

"She's had a very busy day," Lauren explained to the newspaper receptionist.

"I'm glad I made it before you closed." Thelma looked relieved. "My boss Phil is driving me nuts! He said I have to rewrite parts of my article about the pickpocket – said there's some inconsistencies. If you ask me, he's trying to discourage me from writing any stories for the Gazette. He wants to be the only reporter *and* editor!"

"That's too bad. I hope you get the article published." Zoe put down her latte and hopped off the stool. "Hey, what happened with your cold calling businesses in Zeke's Ridge last week? Get any nibbles?"

"You bet I did." Thelma smiled. "That'll show my boss – ha! He couldn't believe it when I sent him three ads for this week's issue – and grumbled about having to pay me commission. But a deal is a deal. That's what I told him."

"I'm glad," Lauren smiled at her. She was also glad she was her own boss.

"Would you like a latte?" Zoe asked. "Or a pumpkin spice marshmallow mocha?" She pointed to the small chalkboard advertising their new beverage. "Or—"

"I wanted to order more treats for cupcake Friday this week." Thelma's gaze strayed to the glass case, where a few cupcakes and Danishes remained. "And maybe I should get one now – I definitely need something after dealing with Phil today."

"Oh?" Lauren picked up the tongs.

"I'll have this one." Thelma pointed to the new daisy cupcake. "And for our order on Friday, can you deliver us six again? Cash on delivery this time – no one else should be dead when you arrive there this week."

Lauren blinked at Thelma, too shocked to say anything. She glanced at Zoe, whose mouth had parted open.

"Sorry, that didn't come out the right way." Thelma shook her head. "I'm just as cut up about Cee Cee's death as everyone else. I can't believe anyone had the nerve to come into the office and kill her – in broad daylight!"

Lauren nodded, mechanically placing the treat into the brown paper bag.

"I think it must have something to do with the gossip column, don't you? I mean, Cee Cee was practically a stranger here in town. Who would even know her to kill her?"

"Who indeed?" Lauren managed.

"Oh, can you make us the same cupcakes this Friday that we had last week?" Thelma asked as she paid for her to-go treat.

"No worries," Zoe piped up.

After Thelma left, Lauren sank onto a stool and stared at her cousin.

"I feel exactly the same way." Zoe nodded. "I think she's the killer!"

CHAPTER 11

"Really?"

"It all fits," Zoe replied. "She was jealous of Cee Cee because Cee Cee got the gossip column and she was an old friend of her boss's wife. And remember how Thelma told us she'd written some small stories before for the Gazette? But how her boss Phil wasn't exactly encouraging her to keep at it?

"True," Lauren replied thoughtfully.

"I bet Thelma thought if she got rid of Cee Cee, she would get the gossip columnist job. Except it hasn't worked out that way for her – yet. No wonder she's mad."

"But she has an alibi," Lauren pointed out. "She was with Phil at the town council. Someone called them with a red hot lead, remember?"

"Allegedly," Zoe replied. "We only have Thelma's word for it that that actually happened. What if she made

the whole thing up, to establish an
alibi for herself?"

Lauren stared at her cousin. "That's
pretty clever thinking."

"Thanks," Zoe sounded modest.

"But even if Thelma did all that,
how did she kill Cee Cee in Phil's
office if she was with Phil at the time?
And was Phil in his office when she
got this "tip"?"

"Hmm." Zoe tapped her cheek. "I'll
have to give that some more
thought."

"And what about Phil's behavior
this afternoon when we went into his
office? He shut his desk drawer pretty
suddenly."

"That's right." Zoe brightened.
"Maybe he's the killer and he was
making sure the evidence he hid in
his drawer was still there."

"What sort of evidence?" Lauren
frowned. "Mitch said Cee Cee was
strangled with the cord from the desk
lamp."

"I know!" Zoe pointed a finger at
her. "Maybe Cee Cee wrote a piece

of gossip that was about him and BAM! he killed her."

"Why would Cee Cee do that?" Lauren looked at her blankly.

"Because … she didn't know it was about him! Remember that weird piece that was in the last column, about a little birdie and whispers. Maybe she wrote something like that because that's what her source told her to write, knowing it was about Phil but Cee Cee didn't, and that's what got her killed. She's only been here a couple of months. She wouldn't be aware of who knows who around here, and who is a real local and who isn't."

"I guess we're not real locals then," Lauren replied. "We've only lived here for about three years."

"True, but your Gramms was a real local," Zoe pointed out. "People might think of you as one by default, and me as well, by default of you. Mrs. Finch is a real local."

"So you think Phil keeps the evidence of killing Cee Cee in his desk drawer?" Lauren queried,

"Possibly." Zoe nodded to herself. "He looked over her column because it sounds like he approves everything before the newspaper goes to print, realized it was about him, didn't run that bit of gossip and killed Cee Cee anyway. And since Cee Cee is dead she can't ask why he didn't publish that tidbit."

"But he has the same alibi as Thelma," Lauren pointed out.

"Unless they were in it together!"

Lauren looked at her skeptically. "Somehow I can't see those two acting together, especially with something as awful as this."

"That's true." Zoe nodded slowly. "They'd probably both try to sell out the other if Mitch started asking them too many questions. Ooh, I bet Thelma would love to blame the whole thing on Phil even if she was part of it, and then she could take over the newspaper!"

"If Phil's wife allowed her to be in charge," Lauren commented.

"Hmm. I also think the real estate guy is a possibility. He's a bit too slick for my taste."

Lauren nodded, then looked at her watch. Five o'clock. She jumped up and locked the door, then started closing the register.

"Awesome!" Zoe started stacking the chairs on the tables.

"Brrt?" Annie lifted her head, slowly opening her green eyes.

"We've just closed the café," Lauren told her.

"Once we tidy up we can go home!" Zoe winked at the feline.

"Brrt!" Annie climbed out of her basket and poked her head in the nearby corner. Then she moved toward her basket, busy sniffing near the edge of it.

"What is it?" Lauren asked.

"Brrt." Annie slid her paw under the basket, lifting it slightly. She wriggled her head under it, wriggled her bottom, and then triumphantly pulled out a piece of white paper. "Brrt!" She patted the white scrap with her paw.

"What have you got?" Zoe zipped over to her. "Can I see?"

"Brrp." *Yes.* Annie pushed the paper over to Zoe.

"It looks like a phone number written in black ink."

Lauren headed over to them. "A landline number maybe." She stared at the numbers scrawled on the paper. "And there's a smudge on the edge of the paper that looks like the same color as the ink used."

"You're right." Zoe frowned. "The number looks familiar, but I can't place it."

"It's Annie's Lost and Found again." Lauren smiled at her fur baby.

"Brrt!"

"But how did it end up under your basket?" Zoe asked.

"Maybe the three cats found it when they were in here earlier," Lauren proposed, "and hid it under there for safekeeping."

"Or maybe AJ or Mrs. Snuggle did that behind Annie's back." Zoe giggled. "Maybe they wanted it to be a surprise for her or wanted to see if she would find it."

"Brrt!" *I bet it was AJ!*

"I bet it was, too." Lauren shared a smile with her fur baby. "We'd better put this somewhere for safe keeping."

"Like the drawer behind the counter."

"Brrt." *Yes.*

"I wonder who could have lost it?" Zoe mused. "Who was in here today? Gus, that real estate guy Bryce, Ms. Tobin, a ton of people at lunchtime—"

"Thelma," Lauren reminded her.

Zoe's brown eyes widened. "Maybe it was her!"

"But she came in after the playdate." Lauren put the scrap of paper in the drawer. "I'll mention it to Mitch tonight."

"Let me know what he says."

***

That evening, Lauren watched her husband spoon up the last mouthful of fluffy chocolate mousse.

"That was great." He smiled in satisfaction. "Thank you."

"Ms. Tobin gave me the idea," she admitted. "I'll have to let her know."

"You can make that any time."

"So, how's the case going?"

When Mitch had come home for dinner that night, he'd looked tired again. Lauren had made sure he ate a good meal first, including hearty beef stew leftovers, and the chocolate mousse.

Annie had been busy eating her dinner, but now she joined them at the kitchen table, hopping up beside Lauren.

"Castern still hasn't caught the pickpocket, despite his boasting that an arrest is imminent." He frowned. "And I don't think I'm getting any closer to catching Cee Cee's killer."

"I'm sorry." She reached out and touched his hand.

"Thanks." He gave her a small smile. "I've interviewed everyone who was close to Cee Cee – Thelma and Phil at the *Gazette*, and Phil's wife Katherine who was friends with her.

Thanks for giving me that tip about Cee Cee and Katherine poring over celebrity gossip in their college days, but it didn't seem to lead anywhere, apart from Katherine thinking of Cee Cee for the gossip column. Since Cee Cee hadn't been in town long, she didn't appear to have made any new friends that we know of."

"What about that new real estate guy Bryce who came into the *Gazette* office after Zoe and I found Cee Cee?"

"I've looked into him. It could be seen as suspicious that two new people move into a small town around the same time and one of them ends up being murdered, but I can't find any history between him and Cee Cee. He was able to account for his movements that morning as well."

Lauren told him about the scrap of paper that Annie had found underneath her basket.

"I'll grab it in the morning. It should be safe in the café overnight."

She filled him in on the playdate that afternoon. He chuckled and shook his head at the trio's antics.

"It sounds like you had a good time, Annie." He looked at her fondly.

"Brrt." *I did.* She yawned, a wide, big yawn that showed all of her pink tongue.

"Maybe Annie is giving us a hint." Lauren rose and gathered the dishes.

"I'll help." Mitch scraped his chair back. "And then I thought we could watch some TV before going to bed."

CHAPTER 12

The next morning, Lauren snapped a photo of the scrap of paper with the strange number written on it before Mitch bagged it and kissed her goodbye.

She and Zoe readied the café for their first customer. Today, Ed was making his popular honeyed walnut pastries as well as cherry pinwheels. He'd told Lauren earlier that AJ had seemed to enjoy her time with Annie and Mrs. Snuggle.

"I think she'd like another playdate with them soon." He'd smiled.

"I'll check with Annie and Mrs. Snuggle." She asked him about the scrap of paper Annie had found, but he'd shaken his shaggy head and said he hadn't dropped anything like that.

Their first customer was Brooke, looking stylish in pale blue jeans and a cream top.

"Sorry I haven't been in earlier this week." She smiled down at Annie who trotted over to her. "Yes, I would like a table today, please." She checked her watch. "I have thirty minutes before my first client."

"Awesome." Zoe grinned. "Lauren's made her new creation today – daisy cupcakes."

Annie led Brooke to a four-seater near the counter and hopped up on a chair next to her. Lauren and Zoe joined them.

"You've got to try our pumpkin spice marshmallow mocha," Zoe urged. "And the new cupcake."

"Okay." Brooke looked intrigued.

"You're going to love both," Zoe promised.

"I hope you do," Lauren added.

"I'm sure I will." Brooke smiled.

Annie kept the hair stylist company while her order was prepared.

"Ooh, that looks good." Zoe peered at the espresso-based concoction as Lauren sprinkled hot chocolate powder on top. "I think I'll have one later."

"Me too," Lauren said, thinking she would go light on the marshmallows for herself. Too many weren't good for her curves.

"I can't wait to try both treats." Brooke's green eyes lit up as they placed the cupcake and coffee in front of her.

"How's business?" Zoe watched their friend plunge a fork into one of the daisies.

"Good, until now," she answered after tasting the fondant flower. "Delicious, Lauren."

"Thanks." She smiled.

"I don't have so many appointments today, so I thought I'd treat myself, and I've been looking forward to trying this new cupcake." She tapped the lilac frosting. "Now I'll test the pumpkin spice." Brooke took a delicate sip, her face lighting up. She sipped again. "This is amazing!"

"Thanks." Zoe grinned, then told her how they'd thought up the new beverage.

"I'll be sure to tell my clients about it – and my husband."

"Awesome!"

"Brrt?" Annie looked from Lauren to Zoe to Brooke, and then over at the counter.

"Oh, that reminds me." Lauren glanced fondly at her fur baby. "Annie found a scrap of paper yesterday afternoon."

"Yeah, and it has a phone number on it."

"Is this your number?" Lauren showed the photo on her phone to Brooke. She glanced at her cousin. "Mitch took the piece of paper to the station this morning."

"No, it's not my number, or the salon's." Their friend looked puzzled. "It seems a little familiar, but I don't know why."

"That's what I said." Zoe nodded. "Ooh, maybe it's the phone number for the senior center!"

"Could be," Lauren replied.

"That's probably it." Brooke's expression cleared, then her eyes widened. She was facing the large window next to the entrance door. "Is that Martha?"

The three of them swiveled to look where she pointed.

"Brrt!" Annie jumped down from the pine chair and ran to the door, stretching up against the glass and peering out.

Martha was talking to someone outside the café, swinging her head wildly from side to side, her small handbag bumping across her body. Her hands gripped each side of her rolling walker.

The person she was speaking to wore sunglasses, dark slacks, and a smart gray jacket. Lauren didn't recognize him.

The three of them joined Annie at the door.

"Stay here," Lauren told the feline, then opened the door. "Martha, are you okay?"

Martha rammed her walker into the stranger. "I'm gonna get you, you – you – horrible pickpocket!" She rammed the walker again, this time connecting with his shin.

"Ow! Ouch! Stop it! I'm sorry!" He hopped backward and nearly fell over on the sidewalk.

"How dare you try to steal my wallet!" Martha ran forward with her walker, as if she were about to trample him with her wheels.

"Martha!" Lauren caught her arm. "What's going on?"

"I can't believe you caught the pickpocket! Awesome!" Zoe grinned. "Detective Castern couldn't do it."

"Are you okay?" Brooke asked in concern.

"Brrt?" Annie had trotted out of the café to join them.

"I'm making a citizen's arrest, that's what's going on." Martha's cheeks were flushed. "You'd better call the cops quick, before I'm tempted to run over him – this time permanently!"

***

Mitch arrived in record time, Detective Castern accompanying him.

"Arrest that man!" Martha cried dramatically, now sitting on her walker outside the café. "He tried to pickpocket me!"

The young man in question blustered, but under the weight of Mitch's and Detective Castern's stares, soon crumbled. Or perhaps it was the way Martha continued to eye him, and he preferred the safety of the police station to the freedom of the sidewalk – and Martha.

Detective Castern led him away in handcuffs, puffed up with self-importance as he did so.

"You'll have to come down to the station later to give a statement," Mitch told Martha. "Unless Detective Castern can make it over here to the café."

"I'll come down," Martha decided, "as soon as I fortify myself with a pumpkin spice marshmallow mocha – that's my new favorite drink, you know."

Mitch smiled, his brown eyes crinkling at the corners. "Take your time. Detective Castern should be at the station all day."

"And your pumpkin spice is on the house," Zoe declared.

"Along with anything you'd like to eat," Lauren added, smiling at Martha in admiration.

"You girls are good to me." She beamed.

They accompanied Martha into the café, Annie sitting on the black vinyl seat and directing them all to a table with a series of brrts and brrps.

"Better make it a large one, Lauren." Martha sank down at a large table, Annie sitting beside her. "And I think I definitely need a cupcake after all that." She suddenly looked pale.

"Of course." Lauren nodded.

"Don't worry," Zoe told her, "we'll make you something good."

Brooke kept the older woman company while Lauren and Zoe bustled behind the counter. Zoe plated two cupcakes – a daisy, and a triple chocolate ganache, while Lauren made a large pumpkin spice.

"Put plenty of marshmallows in," Zoe advised. "I think Martha needs lots of sugar right now."

"Already doing it." She'd already put in a double serve of the mini pink and white treats, knowing how fond Martha was of them – when she wasn't fighting off pickpockets.

"Hey, do you think Detective Castern was right about the pickpocket hanging around outside our café, or do you think he just made it up to annoy us, and got lucky?" Zoe frowned.

"I haven't seen that man before – the one Martha arrested," she replied.

"Me neither. And we've been zipping here and there lately. I'm sure we would have spotted him if he *had* been casing the café – and our customers. Castern must have just had a lucky guess, and it came true today."

"That looks great." Martha grinned at the laden tray when they brought it over. "Lots of marshmallows – goody. And *two* cupcakes?" Her eyes widened as Zoe placed the plate in front of her.

"For doing the town a service and nabbing the pickpocket," she explained.

"Brrt!"

"But how did you know what to do?" Brooke asked.

"I think I got a bit carried away from watching the martial arts demonstration yesterday at the senior center," Martha admitted, placing a big forkful of triple chocolate ganache into her mouth. Her eyes closed in enjoyment as she munched away. "I signed up for lessons but they don't start until next week."

"How did the pickpocket approach you?" Zoe wanted to know.

"I was just about come in here when I felt a tug on my purse and a hand trying to get inside it." She looked chagrined. "I hadn't zipped it up this morning. And then I saw that character attached to the hand dipping into my bag – never seen him before, and I know most people around here – and what the expert told us yesterday about being vigilant flashed through my mind. And I decided he wasn't going to steal from *me*!"

"I think you're going to be awesome at self-defense," Zoe told her.

"Brrt!"

"I think so, too." Lauren smiled.

Mrs. Finch entered the café and Annie ran to her, escorting her to Martha's table.

"Wait until you hear what happened," Zoe said enthusiastically. "Martha caught the pickpocket!"

"My goodness!" Mrs. Finch said in admiration. "You must tell me all about it."

They took Mrs. Finch's order of a pumpkin spice marshmallow mocha and a daisy cupcake. Brooke made her apologies to everyone, promising to tell all her clients about Martha's exploits, and returned to the salon.

When they placed Mrs. Finch's order in front of her, Lauren was struck by a sudden thought. "Do either of you know who this phone number belongs to?" She dug out her phone from her blue capris' pocket and read it out.

"Is it the senior center?" Zoe asked.

"Nope." Martha shook her head. "It's not my number, either."

"Nor mine," Mrs. Finch said.

"Pooh." Zoe drummed her fingers on the table. "We were sure it was the senior center's phone number."

They told their friends how Annie had found the scrap of paper yesterday, the feline joining in with a few brrts.

"Now you have two mysteries to solve," Martha grinned. "Who this phone number belongs to, and who killed Cee Cee."

"Brrt!" *That's right!*

Once Martha was fully fortified, she left to go to the police station and make a statement. Lauren offered to accompany her the short distance, but Martha waved away her help.

"I'll be fine," she insisted. "Once word gets around town that I fought off a criminal, no one will ever think of messing with me again." She grinned.

Mrs. Finch left soon after. Lauren promised to bring her knitting again the following night for craft club, and Zoe said she was busy thinking up a design featuring Annie, AJ, and Mrs. Snuggle for her new mug project.

"You must tell me all about it tomorrow," Mrs. Finch said.

"We will," Zoe replied cheerfully.

Mrs. Finch waved away their offer of accompanying her home, insisting she would be fine. "Perhaps I should sign up for these self-defense classes," she mused.

"I think that's an awesome idea!" Zoe encouraged.

Lauren nodded.

"Brrt!"

***

That afternoon, two of their favorite customers entered – tall, athletic Claire, and her little daughter Molly.

"Brrt!" Annie scampered to greet them.

"Annie!" Molly's blonde curls were tousled around her face as she beamed at Annie in delight.

"Hi, Claire. Hi, Molly." Lauren came over. It had been slow since the lunch rush finished, something she was now glad about. Hopefully they could all sit down together and enjoy each other's company for a few minutes at least.

"Brrt!" *This way.* Annie trotted to a six-seater table near the counter and jumped up on one of the chairs.

Molly plumped down next to her, already talking about her own cat Kitty. When the café had hosted a cat adoption day for the local animal shelter, the little girl had fallen in love with a kitten that looked a lot like Annie.

"How's school?" Lauren inquired.

"Love it!" Molly beamed. "Soon I'll be home with Mommy again!"

"Summer vacation," Claire told them. She looked at her daughter fondly. "I can't believe how much I missed her when she started school."

"Big school," Molly insisted, gently petting Annie with "fairy pats".

The three of them chuckled.

"What can I get both of you?" Lauren asked.

"I'd love to try your new pumpkin spice coffee," Claire requested. "And your new cupcake – if it's available."

"It definitely is." Zoe nodded.

"And a cino! Pwease," Molly added.

Molly asked for a babycino every time she visited. Made from steamed milk froth, with mini marshmallows and a sprinkle of hot chocolate powder, her enjoyment was always evident.

When they brought the order over to them, Molly eagerly looked at the tray.

"Yum!" She took her first sip of the cino, a little smear of marshmallow and milk froth decorating her upper lip.

"This looks wonderful." Claire admired the daisy cupcake and pumpkin spice mocha.

"Molly have some?" The little girl's eyes widened as she looked at the pretty daisy flowers on the cake.

"Just a little." Claire used the fork to divide the treat in two and gave her the smaller half.

Lauren and Zoe had already anticipated Molly's request, supplying two plates and forks.

"Yummy!" Molly smacked her lips after the first bite. "Pwetty flowers." She beamed at all of them, chewing on one of the fondant petals.

"How is your screenplay coming along, Zoe?" Claire took a sip of the pumpkin spice, her eyes widening. "This is different – but I like it."

"Thanks." Lauren and Zoe said at the same time.

Zoe filled her in on yesterday's feline play date, Annie adding her own comments in a series of brrts and brrps. Then they quickly told her about Martha apprehending the pickpocket, choosing their words carefully in case Molly was listening.

Molly slurped her babycino, then put the small cup down as a thought struck her. "Can Annie come play with me and Kitty?" She looked pleadingly at her mother and then Annie.

"Brrt!" *Yes!*

Now it was Annie's turn to look hopefully at Lauren.

Lauren and Claire exchanged glances.

"It's fine with me," Lauren began, "if it's okay with you, Claire."

"That's what I was about to say." Claire laughed. "We'll have to set up a date that suits everyone."

"Goody!" Molly gently hugged Annie. "We'll have lots of fun!"

"Brrt!" Annie nodded in agreement.

Lauren and Claire discussed some possible dates, settling on Saturday afternoon the following weekend.

"Can't wait, Annie!" Molly beamed at the feline, her mouth now smeared with pink marshmallow and hot chocolate powder.

Claire showed them the latest photos of Molly and Kitty, promising to take some of Annie as well at the upcoming play date.

A few more customers entered, and Lauren made her apologies. Zoe joined her in serving the newcomers, while Annie seated them and returned to Molly and Claire.

When the mother-daughter duo left, the little girl beamed. "Annie's coming to my house!"

CHAPTER 13

"Craft club tonight," Zoe sang out, unstacking the chairs in the café. "How's your blanket coming along, Lauren?"

"Very slowly." She hadn't worked on it at all that week and now felt guilty. "Hopefully I can make some progress on it tonight."

"And I need to start making sketches of Annie, AJ, and Mrs. Snuggle. I called Father Mike and Ed last night and they both said they were thrilled about my new mug design idea."

"That's great." Lauren looked up from the register and smiled.

"Brrt!" *Yes!*

They finished getting the space ready.

"Don't forget, one of us needs to deliver the cupcakes to the newspaper office." Lauren boxed up the order and placed it to one side.

"Ten o'clock, right?" Zoe confirmed.

"Yes. I think one of us should stay and mind the café."

"I'll stay and you go," Zoe suggested. "Annie and I will be in charge." She winked at the feline.

"Brrt!"

Ms. Tobin came in after they opened, and ordered a large latte. Annie kept her company, chattering away to her, while Lauren made the coffee.

Zoe updated her on Martha's citizen's arrest of the pickpocket, something Ms. Tobin hadn't heard about.

When Gus walked in a few minutes later, Annie peered over at him. Lauren wondered if she was torn between being a good hostess or wanting to continue to sit with Ms. Tobin.

He solved the problem by striding up to the counter, ignoring the *Please Wait to be Seated* sign.

"Can I grab a few cupcakes to go?" he asked. "I told my wife about them and she said I should bring some home today for her and Brian."

"Of course. Which ones would you like?"

He eyed the blueberry cream, triple chocolate ganache, and Norwegian apple offerings. "How about one of each?"

Lauren nodded, boxing up the selection.

As he handed her some cash, she said, "That reminds me. We – well, Annie – found a piece of paper on the floor with what looks like a phone number."

She dug out her phone, suddenly remembering that earlier that morning Mitch had told her he'd discovered who that phone number belonged to, but before he could say any more, his phone had buzzed, summoning him to the station. The pickpocket had decided to admit to all of his crimes, including targeting Detective Castern.

Zoe emerged from the kitchen, the doors swinging behind her. "Ed wants to know if he can get off work a few minutes earlier today because they're short-handed at the shelter again."

"No problem," Lauren replied absently, finding the photo.

"I keep forgetting there's some sort of ink splodge on the edge of that paper scrap." Zoe peered over Lauren's shoulder.

She showed the photo to Gus.

"It's not my number." He shook his head. "Can't say I've seen it before." He frowned.

"Huh." Zoe grabbed the phone from Lauren and studied it. "I'm sure I know that number from somewhere. I'll definitely have to think about it. I bet this could be a real clue."

"As to who the pickpocket is?" Gus inquired, picking up the cupcake box.

"Martha arrested him yesterday." Zoe giggled. "I hope I'm as awesome as her when I'm that age."

"I think you will be." Lauren smiled at her cousin.

"Really? He's been arrested?" Gus looked surprised.

"It happened right outside here." Zoe gestured to the sidewalk visible from the entrance door.

"And it sounds like he's confessing to everything," Lauren added.

"That's good." Gus nodded. "We don't want any crime around here."

"We definitely don't," Zoe agreed.

He waved goodbye and strode down the sidewalk.

"Oh!" Lauren made a face. "We forgot to show Claire the phone number yesterday."

"That's right." Zoe tapped her cheek. "We'll ask her when she comes in next time."

Lauren nodded and checked her watch.

"I've got to deliver these cupcakes." She patted the cardboard box.

"Go," Zoe urged. "Annie and I have got things covered." She glanced over at the silver-gray tabby, who was listening thoughtfully to Ms. Tobin.

"Thanks." Lauren picked up the box and headed to the newspaper office. Her errand should only take a minute.

When she reached the cream and peach Victorian house, she entered the office and smiled at Thelma. "Here are your cupcakes."

"Thanks." The receptionist rose and banged on the inner door. "Cupcakes are here," she hollered. "I need the cash to pay Lauren."

Phil opened the door and stuck his head out.

"Thanks," he said gruffly, handing Thelma a wad of cash. He nodded to Lauren and shut the door again.

Thelma rolled her eyes. "As I don't know what he's doing in there," she muttered to herself.

Lauren couldn't help herself. "What *is* he doing?" She remembered the way he'd slammed shut the desk drawer the other day when she and Zoe had poked their heads into his inner office.

Thelma glanced around, as if expecting to see an eavesdropper, and then lowered her voice.

"Scratch cards."

Lauren blinked.

"You know, those instant lottery cards. You scratch off the picture and it reveals whether you've won a prize. He promised his wife he'd stop buying them, as he never wins anything, and it's starting to cost him a fortune, but I caught him at it again the other day." She tsked. "He thinks I didn't notice. That's because I have all the makings of an investigative journalist." She nodded to herself.

"That's why I was so peeved when the boss hired Cee Cee to write the gossip column." She leaned across the desk. "Did you know that she made up one item of gossip? Total fiction!"

"Really?"

"Uh-huh." Thelma opened her desk drawer and pulled out a cutting.

"A little birdie told me echoed whispers often come to a dead end." Her voice was dramatic. "Can you believe it?" Thelma reverted to her normal tone. "She said she felt guilty doing it, but she was up against a deadline and had space she needed to fill in. She asked me not to tell Phil."

"Did you?" Lauren asked.

"Nope." Thelma smirked. "It wouldn't bother me if that came back to bite him in the you-know-where. It would show him that he shouldn't have hired her."

"Did you hear that Martha caught the pickpocket?"

"Indeed I did. I found out yesterday when I was at the police station for an update on the sitch. That means situation," she told Lauren kindly. "I'm going to write a full piece about Martha apprehending him. By the time I'm finished, everyone in town will know Martha's name and I'll make sure Phil publishes it because otherwise—" she ran her finger across her throat.

"Otherwise?" Lauren echoed, her eyes widening.

"I'll threaten to tell his wife about his little scratch card habit starting up again. But it won't be a threat."

"Oh," Lauren said faintly. She checked the money Thelma handed her, wanting to take only the correct amount, but the receptionist insisted she take the couple of extra dollars, saying that was how much her boss wanted to pay her, and why quibble about a little more?

"I might want to make cupcake Friday a permanent thing." Thelma plucked a triple chocolate ganache from the box and broke off a piece. "These are so good."

"Thanks." Lauren tucked the money into her wallet. "I hope you and Phil enjoy them."

"If I don't eat them all first." Thelma chuckled. The phone rang and she picked up the receiver with a chocolatey hand.

Lauren returned to the café. Ms. Tobin had departed, but Zoe was busy steaming milk for a cappuccino. Annie escorted a customer to a small table in the middle of the room, then climbed into her basket.

"Oh, good." Zoe grinned at her. "Can you plate two apple Danishes and a blueberry cream, please?"

"Right away boss," she teased. Usually, Zoe called her boss.

The morning flew by, Lauren updating Zoe about Phil's scratch card habit, Cee Cee making up the little birdie item in the gossip column, and Thelma knowing about Martha's citizen's arrest in snatches.

"That reminds me," Zoe told her when they had a brief lull and sat on stools behind the counter. "I called Father Mike while you were at the *Gazette* office, and checked with Ed. AJ and Mrs. Snuggle are coming over straight after we close today for a quick sketching session."

Lauren looked at her blankly. "But we've got craft club tonight."

"I know, but this will probably take thirty minutes or so. Still plenty of time to have a quick dinner and be punctual for Mrs. Finch."

"Okay. Have you told Annie?"

"Brrt!" *Yes!* Annie called from her pink basket, sitting up straight.

Lauren smiled at her fur baby.

The afternoon was just as busy as the morning. Lauren was looking forward to relaxing at craft club, but hopefully she could manage to knit a few rows of her blanket as well.

When five o'clock arrived, Zoe was already stacking chairs on tables.

"Is this a good time?" Ed poked his head through the kitchen door. "I've got AJ outside."

"Perfect." Zoe smiled. "I'll only be a minute."

"You might as well start your sketching session now," Lauren said. She'd noticed Annie's ears pricked up at the mention of AJ.

"You're not volunteering at the shelter tonight?" Zoe asked him.

"No." He shook his shaggy auburn head. "Just me and AJ. Rebecca is having a girls' night out with some friends." He paused. "I think AJ wants to watch the princess movie again."

"Awesome!" Zoe giggled.

Father Mike arrived with Mrs. Snuggle, both men promising to come back in about forty minutes to pick up their felines.

"Thanks for letting me sketch them," Zoe said, her brown eyes sparkling.

"Thank *you*," Father Mike replied. "I'm sure Mrs. Snuggle will be proud to be on one of your mugs."

"AJ too." Ed nodded.

Lauren shooed Zoe into the cottage, along with the three cats.

"I promise I'll come in early tomorrow to finish tidying up." Zoe waved a hand toward the unvacuumed floor.

"I'll fix it," Lauren promised, already thinking that in the morning she would bake her three simplest cupcakes. She was already looking forward to tomorrow afternoon when she would be able to just relax in the cottage with Annie – and hopefully Mitch – if he wasn't required at the station.

Lauren quickly vacuumed and took care of the few dishes remaining in the kitchen. Ed always left his workspace clean and tidy, which she appreciated.

By the time she finished, it was almost five-thirty. Time to join the sketching party.

Zoe had lined up the three cats on the pink sofa in the living room.

"That's perfect, Mrs. Snuggle," she praised.

The fluffy white Persian sat up straight, her head titled to one side as if she thought *she* was a princess.

"How's it going?" she asked.

"I've already taken Annie's portrait." Zoe flipped through her sketch book.

Lauren smiled at her fur baby's likeness, looking like a princess herself. It was amazing how good Zoe was at drawing.

"All she needs is a crown."

"Brrt!" *Yes!*

"Meow!" Mrs. Snuggle added a little demandingly.

"I think Mrs. Snuggle just said me too," Zoe murmured.

"I think you're right." Lauren tried not to giggle.

"Meow!" AJ didn't want to be left out.

"And you also, AJ," Zoe replied. "Now, I'll just finish off Mrs. Snuggle's portrait, and then I'll start on yours." She smiled at the Maine Coon.

"Will you have enough time?" Lauren furrowed her brow.

"It took a bit longer than I thought to get them sitting on the sofa at the same time," Zoe whispered. "They all wanted a snack, and then AJ started playing with the jingle balls."

The doorbell chimed.

"I hope it's not Ed or Father Mike." Zoe frowned. "I haven't finished my sketches."

"I'll go." Lauren hurried to open the door and blinked at the person standing on the doorstep. "Gus?"

"Hi, Lauren. Sorry to bother you." Gus nodded. His T-shirt had a couple of oil stains on it. "I stopped by the café and it was closed, but I heard you lived next door."

"That's right. What can I do for you?"

"My wife and son loved the cupcakes I bought them and I wanted to get some more."

"I'm afraid all the cupcakes and Danishes have sold out but I can set some aside for you tomorrow. We're open until lunchtime."

"Could you write down my order? It's a bit of a complicated one."

"Okay. I'll just grab a piece of paper." She'd left her phone in the kitchen so she couldn't make a note on it. Feeling awkward at leaving him standing on the doorstep, she said, "Would you like to come in for a second?"

"Thanks." He stepped inside.

"Brrt?" Annie appeared behind her, her silver-gray brow wrinkled. Mrs. Snuggle and AJ appeared by their friend's side.

"Are these all your cats?" Gus's eyes widened.

"No, only Annie. Mrs. Snuggle and AJ are friends of hers."

"I'm sketching them." Zoe appeared behind the cats. "AJ, I can start on your portrait now."

"Are you a painter?" he asked.

"No, but I'm making pottery mugs for the café and our customers," Zoe told him enthusiastically. "I've already got Ms. Tobin down for my – our–" she glanced at Lauren and then the cats "–first sale."

"I'll have to tell my wife." His chuckle sounded a little forced.

"Are you okay?" Lauren asked. "Would you like a glass of water?"

"Yeah, water would be good." He followed her down the hall to the kitchen. "Hey, did you find out who that phone number belonged to? I've been racking my brain all day about it."

"No, I'm afraid not." She got out a glass and filled it up, noticing Annie still by her side. "Here you go."

"Thanks." He took a healthy swallow and placed it on the table with a small bang. "Sorry."

"What sort of cupcakes would you like for tomorrow?" Lauren reached for a piece of paper, which was closer to her than her phone. "I was thinking of making lemon poppy seed, lavender, and Norwegian apple."

"Sounds good." He nodded. "How about two of each?"

"Of course." She made a note.

"Hey, Lauren!" Zoe zoomed into the kitchen along with AJ and Mrs. Snuggle. "I know who owns that phone number! Chris just texted me and I was glancing at my contacts and it's …."

"Don't leave us in suspense," Lauren teased.

"It's the newspaper office! The *Gold Leaf Valley Gazette!* Remember when I called Thelma to tell her about the pickpocket?"

"Brrt." Annie's tone was a low warning. She bunted Lauren's ankle.

She looked down at her fur baby, and crinkled her brow.

"And I've been thinking all day about that smudge on the edge of the scrap of paper." Zoe tapped her cheek. She glanced at Lauren, and then Gus, then Lauren, then Gus, this time zeroing in on the oil stains on his T-shirt and his freshly scrubbed fingers. "I bet it's—" Her eyes widened and she gave Lauren a frantic look.

"You bet it's what?" Gus's voice was suddenly menacing.

"Nothing," Zoe said. "I have to get back to sketching AJ." She reached her hand into her jeans' pocket but came up empty. "I left my phone in the living room."

Lauren made a sudden grab for her phone on the kitchen table, but Gus beat her to it.

"Not so fast." He glowered.

"Brrt!" Annie's fur rose. So did AJ's and Mrs. Snuggle's. They'd joined their friend, who stood beside Lauren.

"It was you!" Zoe pointed at him. "*You* killed Cee Cee!"

"Gus?" Lauren stared at him and took a step back. "Why?"

"You wouldn't understand."

"We might," Zoe said.

"I'm sure Mitch would," Lauren added. "Why don't I call him and ask him to come over? I know he'd give you a fair hearing."

"No." Gus vigorously shook his head. "Not happening. Why do you think I killed Cee Cee? No one is going to ruin my new life, including you two." He took a menacing step forward.

"Brrt." It was a growl. Annie's fur puffed up and she stared at Gus with piercing green eyes.

Mrs. Snuggle looked just as fierce, and the grumpiest Lauren had ever seen her, which was saying something.

And AJ looked like she was hangry and he was a convenient snack she wanted to eat.

"Get these cats out of here." He flapped his hands. "Go on. Shoo."

"They won't leave until we tell them to." Lauren hoped she wasn't bluffing about AJ and Mrs. Snuggle.

"Yeah, you're stuck with them. Just like we're stuck with you." Zoe glowered.

"The best thing for you to do is hand yourself in. Maybe they'll go easy on you," Lauren told him.

"No, they won't. They don't go easy on killers. And that's what I am – thanks to Cee Cee."

"Why don't you tell us about it?" She hoped he would relax enough so she could grab her phone – or something to use as a weapon. Her heart hammered hard in her chest and she drew in a deep breath to try and steady herself. She glanced at Zoe, who seemed to be doing the same thing.

"It's all her fault," he burst out. "Why couldn't she leave things alone – *me* alone?"

"What did she do?" Zoe asked.

"Cee Cee made it plain she was talking about me in the gossip column – "*A little birdie told me echoed whispers often come to a dead end*" – she was talking about me!"

"Umm, I don't think she was," Lauren said.

"Yeah, Thelma said she made that up. That's what Lauren told me this morning."

"No, Cee Cee didn't." Gus scowled. "Because I bumped into her the day after that column came out and I asked her where she got her information from, and she just tapped her nose and said, "I have my sources." And she laughed!"

"Maybe she didn't want you asking awkward questions," Zoe commented.

"Thelma said Cee Cee admitted to her she made that item up because she was on a deadline and needed something else for her column," Lauren added. "It wasn't about you."

"Arggh!" He clutched his head. "I was so sure she was talking about *me*!"

"What did you do?" Zoe asked curiously.

"Brrt," Annie added gravely.

"I used to work in a chop shop in LA. It was the only job I could get. I have a wife, and two kids in college I try to help out. I didn't approve of what the chop shop guys were doing, but I thought it probably didn't matter as long as no one got hurt."

He paused.

"Did someone get hurt?" Lauren asked.

"An eighteen-year-old boy bought one of our cars and died in a crash. I knew it was because of that car. I warned my boss that some of the parts we were using were too old to last long but he said it didn't matter as long as the car sold. So when I heard about that boy, I quit, and my wife and I moved here."

"But why Gold Leaf Valley?" Zoe asked.

"I found an old workshop that was cheap to rent and after the hustle and bustle of LA, it was nice to live somewhere a lot slower. And I was the only mechanic here. So I decided to set up my own shop, do honest work and charge reasonable prices. And it was going really well. We even applied to foster a kid, and they gave us Brian. He's a good boy. I was trying to atone for what happened in LA."

"Did your wife know about the chop shop?" Lauren asked.

"No." He shook his head. "She would have told me to quit in a heartbeat."

"You phoned in that red hot lead that got Thelma and Phil out of the office!" Zoe pointed a finger at him.

"Yeah," he admitted. "I wrote the *Gazette's* phone number on a piece of paper and used a payphone to call them so they couldn't trace it. Then I put the piece of paper back in my wallet." He scowled. "It must have fallen out of there when I was in your café and your cat—" he looked at all three cats still examining him "—cats found it. And then you two had to go poking your nose in asking everyone who the number belonged to, and then you worked out just now that it was a grease smudge on the edge of the paper."

"But nobody saw you in the newspaper office," Lauren said, desperate to keep him talking. What were they going to do? His arms looked strong and muscular from years of fixing cars. And Cee Cee hadn't stood a chance with him.

"I got lucky. I was hoping Cee Cee was there on her own. If she wasn't, I was going to say I wanted to put my ad in for an extra few weeks. I told her that her boss Phil had an envelope for me in his office, and I followed her in there and—" he mimed wrapping a cord around someone's neck.

Lauren paled. So did Zoe.

"And now it's your turn." He took a step toward them, his eyes narrowing.

Annie's hackles rose. So did AJ's and Mrs. Snuggle's.

She cast a sideways glance at Zoe, then down at Annie, AJ, and Mrs. Snuggle. Spying the three food bowls near her feet, an idea began to form.

Looking down at the bowl, and then at the cats, she hoped the felines would pick up on her silent idea. Would Mrs. Snuggle remember that she had once attacked a man's ankles?

Out of the corner of her eye, she caught Zoe doing the same thing, and her spirits lifted. Surely the five of them could foil Gus?

"Brrt!" Annie darted toward Gus. So did AJ and Mrs. Snuggle.

"Shoo!" He shifted his feet and flapped his hands.

AJ pushed one of the bowls toward him, and Annie and Mrs. Snuggle dashed behind him and attacked the back of his ankles.

"Ow! Stop!" He stumbled toward the bowl AJ had conveniently placed before him. Lauren and Zoe stuck out their feet. "Arrgh!" He tripped and fell, his face landing in one of the bowls. A faint smear of gravy decorated his cheek when he managed to lift his head.

"Brrt!" Annie pounced on his back with a thud. So did AJ and Mrs. Snuggle.

"You girls are awesome!" Zoe's eyes lit up. She turned to Lauren. "I'll keep an eye on him and you call Mitch."

Lauren had already snatched up her phone with shaking fingers and speed-dialed him. While she spoke to her husband, she spied Zoe lifting the grill pan from the stove and holding it menacingly over Gus's head.

"One move from you and …" Zoe mimed hitting him on the head.

"Get them off," Gus pleaded. "They're really hurting me!"

"By sitting on a strong man like you?" Zoe eyed him skeptically. "Not a chance. You'll try to kill us – again."

Lauren finished her call and glanced at the cats, noticing how proudly each large feline sat on Gus's back – so straight and tall, and not giving him a chance to move.

"Thank you." She grasped the corner of the table to steady herself. "All of you."

"Brrt!" *You're welcome!*

"Meow!" AJ replied.

"Meow!" Mrs. Snuggle added.

It sounded like they were saying, "*You're welcome*" as well.

Mitch and uniformed officers arrived at the same time as Father Mike and Ed.

The three cats kept a watchful eye on Gus until he was in handcuffs. Then Mrs. Snuggle ran to Father Mike and demanded to be picked up, and AJ dashed to Ed and leapt up on him.

Lauren sank onto a chair and cuddled Annie.

"Are you okay?" Mitch sat down next to her and wrapped an arm around her.

"I am." She smiled. "Thanks to Annie, AJ, and Mrs. Snuggle."

"Hey, don't forget me," Zoe teased. "I helped trip him over too, and threatened him with the grill pan."

"Brrt!"

EPILOGUE

"But I wanted the killer to be Bryce, the real estate guy," Zoe complained the next evening. "There's something about him that's a bit too slick."

The five of them were having dinner around Zoe and Chris's vintage Formica kitchen table. They'd just finished their main course of garlic steak and mushrooms, cooked to perfection courtesy of Zoe and the new air fryer, and accompanied with a green salad.

"I looked into Bryce thoroughly," Mitch assured her. "Maybe he can't help being a bit like that."

"And maybe Gold Leaf Valley will help rub that slickness off him," Chris said thoughtfully. "I love living here." He'd moved from Sacramento to be closer to Zoe when they were dating.

"I think we all do." Lauren shared a smile with Mitch.

"Brrt!" *Yes!*

They all chuckled.

"So what's going to happen to Gus?" Zoe asked. "And the pickpocket?"

"Detective Castern is throwing the book at the pickpocket because he's still embarrassed he didn't notice the guy got his wallet. And Gus will be going away for a while."

"What about his wife and Brian, his foster son?" Lauren asked.

"Hopefully she'll be able to keep looking after him. They're going to live with her sister in Sacramento who has a good job and has promised to help her find one with a part-time schedule, so she can still be there for Brian."

"That's good." Zoe nodded.

After a moment, Lauren asked, "Have you two decided on a honeymoon destination?"

"Yes." Zoe glanced at Chris.

"You tell them."

"Puerto Rico!"

"I'm sure you'll have a great time." Lauren smiled.

"Brrt!"

"I'm glad I decided to put my money toward our honeymoon, and not buy the car, even after Gus painted it Zoe red." Zoe gave a little shudder. "I think I'd feel icky every time I drove her, knowing I bought her from a killer."

"Maybe that's why you sensed there was something not quite right about the car even after he painted it," Lauren suggested.

"You could be right." Zoe's expression brightened.

"Was the ad you placed in the *Gazette* last week profitable?" Chris asked Lauren.

"I think we came out even," she replied.

"We couldn't compete with the martial arts demonstration at the senior center," Zoe added.

"But Thelma's considering putting in a regular order for cupcake Friday," Lauren commented.

Zoe stretched in her chair. "Catching a killer can be exhausting," she admitted, "but I'm looking forward to visiting Mrs. Finch after church tomorrow and telling her what happened."

"It's a shame we had to cancel craft club last night," Lauren added. They'd called Mrs. Finch to let her know they wouldn't be able to make it because of their confrontation with Gus, and having to record their statements.

"But she said she's looking forward to seeing us tomorrow and hearing all about it. Isn't that right, Annie?" Zoe winked at the feline.

"Brrt!"

THE END

I hope you enjoyed reading this mystery. Sign up to my newsletter at www.JintyJames.com and be among the first to discover when my next book is published!

Please turn the page for a list of all my books.

TITLES BY JINTY JAMES

Purrs and Peril – A Norwegian Forest Cat Café Cozy Mystery – Book 1

Meow Means Murder - A Norwegian Forest Cat Café Cozy Mystery – Book 2

Whiskers and Warrants - A Norwegian Forest Cat Café Cozy Mystery – Book 3

Two Tailed Trouble – A Norwegian Forest Cat Cafe Cozy Mystery – Book 4

Paws and Punishment – A Norwegian Forest Cat Café Cozy Mystery – Book 5

Kitty Cats and Crime – A Norwegian Forest Cat Café Cozy Mystery – Book 6

Pouncing on the Proof – A Norwegian Forest Cat Café Cozy Mystery – Book 14

Fur Babies and Forgery – A Norwegian Forest Cat Café Cozy Mystery – Book 15

Leaping into Larceny – A Norwegian Forest Cat Café Cozy Mystery – Book 16

<u>Maddie Goodwell Series (fun witch cozies)</u>

Spells and Spiced Latte - A Coffee Witch Cozy Mystery - Maddie Goodwell 1

Visions and Vanilla Cappuccino - A Coffee Witch Cozy Mystery - Maddie Goodwell 2

Magic and Mocha – A Coffee Witch Cozy Mystery – Maddie Goodwell 3

Enchantments and Espresso – A Coffee Witch Cozy Mystery – Maddie Goodwell 4

Familiars and French Roast - A Coffee Witch Cozy Mystery – Maddie Goodwell 5

Incantations and Iced Coffee – A Coffee Witch Cozy Mystery – Maddie Goodwell 6

Printed in Great Britain
by Amazon

28809256R00142